THE ART OF LOVE

Hazel Crick is furious when her entry for the Town Art Show is rejected. Convinced her colleague Jon Hunter is responsible, she accuses him of vetoing her painting out of spite. Later that day, she waits beside Jon's car to apologise. But this puts her in the wrong place at the wrong time — she is grabbed, bound, gagged, and bundled into Jon's car — unbeknownst to him. The two are about to be flung together in a hair-raising European adventure . . .

ANNE HOLMAN

THE ART OF LOVE

Complete and Unabridged

LINFORD
Leicester

First published in Great Britain in 2016

First Linford Edition
published 2017

A catalogue record for this book is available
from the British Library.

ISBN 978–1–4448–3328–7

Published by
F. A. Thorpe (Publishing)
Anstey, Leicestershire

Set by Words & Graphics Ltd.
Anstey, Leicestershire
Printed and bound in Great Britain by
T. J. International Ltd., Padstow, Cornwall

This book is printed on acid-free paper

1

'*Oh no!*' Her scream was silent to all but herself in the crowded room.

Hazel Crick wasn't sure whether she was more angry or hurt as she picked up her painting from the rejection box at the Art Exhibition. She tried to hide it as she tucked it under her arm and hurriedly made her way through the crowds towards the town hall's exit.

Visitors, chatting and laughing as they milled around the hall, admiring the pictures on display, made Hazel feel like a miserable outcast. Thundering in her brain was the question: *Why have the Selection Committee refused to exhibit my work of art? What is so unsuitable about my picture that they turned their thumbs down when it was being considered for a place in the exhibition?*

Hazel felt like crying with disappointment — but she was a sensible twenty-four-year-old, and knew she was no Leonardo da Vinci or Picasso. But she'd always enjoyed painting, and had been considered good at art since her youth — winning her school's art prize and obtained the highest grade in her art exams. So why had her painting been rejected? What had the other artists achieved that had made their work better than hers?

Hazel's pixie face was rosy with embarrassment at the thought of anyone asking her why she was taking her painting home. She kept her head down as she ran nimbly down the main staircase to get out of the building with her work — hoping she'd not meet anyone who knew her. Unfortunately, she'd told several people she was going to enter her painting for the newly created Town Art Show. Now she wished she hadn't, and had kept her mouth shut. She dreaded meeting anyone who knew she had entered the competition . . .

She wondered if it could have been

what she painted — the family cat reclining on the sofa, with soft evening light coming through the window and making colourful patterns on the furnishings. No, indeed — her watercolour picture was delightful, and she'd hoped a cat lover might have liked it and bought it. Outside the Town Hall, waiting at the bus stop, she frowned as she tried to puzzle out why her work was considered unsuitable.

For some reason, the District Council's recently-appointed Environmental, Leisure and Cultural Officer, Jon Hunter, came into her mind. From the first time they'd met, she'd taken a dislike to his overconfident attitude, and felt sure he'd probably swayed the committee's decision to reject her painting. Ever since he'd come to the town, she heard he'd dominated any decision made about the town's artistic activities.

Well, Jon Hunter disliked her, and obviously her painting too. Although, come to think of it, he had encouraged her to enter the competition — probably so that he could have the satisfaction of rejecting her work!

She sniffed, and quickly found her hanky to pat her face dry as she raced along. Maybe she was being a bit dramatic — but, looking back, it seemed to be the only logical reason for her artwork to be rejected.

⋆ ⋆ ⋆

She remembered the first time he'd come into the newly-constructed Highminster Community College building, just after the war, where she worked as the principal's private secretary. He'd barged into her office, barely knocking on the door, although its plaque stating 'Private' was plain enough to see.

Hazel had looked up from her work and been taken aback by the strikingly good-looking man, feeling as if she didn't want to take her eyes off him. Such a stunningly handsome man was an unusual sight in the sleepy town of Highminster.

His long legs marched towards her desk.

'I want these posters put up around the college,' he said brusquely, taking a large pile of papers out of his briefcase, which he plonked on Hazel's desk.

Incensed that he hadn't said 'Good Morning' — or even 'Excuse me interrupting your work' — Hazel blinked.

'Oh, do you?' she mouthed, flabbergasted that he could be so direct. Who did he think he was, giving her orders?

'I'll give you twenty posters to put up around the college — you can have more if you ring my secretary.'

Hazel, still sitting at her desk, swished a lock of her long fair hair behind her ear. Then she said crossly as he snapped closed his briefcase, 'Take them away. I don't want your paperwork left on my desk, Mr. Whoever-You-Are. I'm the principal's secretary, and I haven't time to go around the college putting up your posters. Ask one of the students to do it for you.'

Their blue eyes met — it was like a clash of steel. He was obviously used to dishing out orders and having them obeyed. But Hazel, although her slenderness and youthful appearance made her look like a teenager, was no pushover. While he seemed to be taken aback momentarily by her challenging his request (which had sounded more like a command), Hazel firmly closed her teeth, determined not to allow this monster to swallow her.

'What's your name?' he demanded loudly.

She replied quietly, 'Miss Crick. What's yours?'

Surprised, he rubbed his chin, regarding her with vague amusement. 'Mr. Hunter,' he replied. 'I'm the council's newly-appointed Environmental, Leisure and Culture Officer.'

'Oh yes,' Hazel said putting her fingers up to her forehead as if remembering, then she swung around on her swivel chair to reach to her filing cabinet, and took out a file. Rummaging through until she came to a certain piece of paper, she withdrew and scanned it. 'Now, I do recollect the principal having notification about your appointment, Mr. Hunter. Here's the letter. I see you have just been demobbed from the army. You're not married, and have taken lodgings in the town.'

Annoyance registered on his face. 'I thought personal information was supposed to be private?'

Hazel forced herself to smile a little. 'I think I told you: I am the principal's private secretary. I have records on all the staff and students.'

'And so I should have asked you to give me permission for a few notices to be displayed around the college, eh?'

Hazel blushed under his scrutiny as she pressed her lips together tightly. He was making an issue over something that was his problem, not hers. But before she could reply, he'd breathed heavily, and for a moment his presence almost frightened her. He raised his voice and said, 'All right, I haven't the time to argue with you, Miss Crick. If you are too busy to help me, I'll take the posters and put them up myself. Can you let me have some drawing pins or sticky tape?'

Hazel could have claimed that she hadn't even a paperclip to spare — so soon after the war, things were in short supply — but she hesitated. Wasn't she in danger of being impolite? Indeed, she suddenly realized that her manners towards him were not much better than his towards her. She could have offered to put up a few posters for him, couldn't she?

She felt ashamed about her brusque behaviour, but more than that, she realized that she was irresistibly affected by his good looks, and felt she didn't want to annoy him further. So she took a box of drawing pins from her desk drawer and offered them to him, saying, 'Here you are. Please bring back what you don't use — our office supplies are still rationed.'

He replied, 'Thank you, Miss Crick,'

with a slight twist of humour showing on his lips. As she gave him the pins, her fingers accidentally brushed his warm hand, and her heart gave a double beat — it was a wonder he didn't hear it!

Fortunately, he seemed unaware of her quiet gasp, saying, 'Naturally I'll return any pins I don't use. I appreciate what an *efficient* secretary you are — a good stock-keeper, too.' He grinned, almost menacingly.

Who *was* this man? Her hackles up, Hazel felt he was mocking her, and didn't like it. Ignoring him, she turned her back on him and put his file away in the cabinet.

He gave a snort of dissatisfaction, saying, 'Although I have some vitally important work to do, I suppose I must rush and get this lot up on display.' He glanced at his watch before he grabbed the pile of posters and his briefcase. His long, straight legs walked easily towards the door. But before he let himself out, he turned to her and called out, 'These notices are about an art show I'm organizing. Are you interested in art, Miss Crick?'

Hazel's mouth parted and her eyes widened; he had caught her attention. 'Yes, Mr. Hunter, indeed I am. I like to paint in watercolours.'

'Then you'd better get painting — the show is early next month. I look forward to seeing what you can do.'

'I may well do that, Mr. Hunter.'

Having caught her attention like a killer with its prey in its teeth, he smiled — a triumphant smile that lit up his stern expression and warmed her inside. The door clicked shut and he was gone.

Hazel sat and buried her face in her hands. What had got into her? She wasn't usually flummoxed and rude to people. Just the opposite! She normally showed a lot of patience, especially with some of the staff — who, like some of the students, could be difficult at times. But she soon forgot any differences she had with any of them.

However, Mr. Hunter was unforgettable. He'd unsettled her — pierced her

10

private world in some way. And she both liked it — and yet didn't. No man had ever done that before; not even her first kisses had made any lasting impression on her.

Hazel decided perhaps it was because she had a bit of a headache — it was near the end of the working day, and she was tired; she supposed that must be the reason. And the beginning of the college year in October was always a busy time for the principal — and her.

★ ★ ★

Jon Hunter chuckled as he left her office. He liked girls with spirit — and pretty little Miss Crick certainly had plenty of that. He knew, in his hurry to get the job done, he'd riled her a bit — although she was not the friendliest secretary he'd met. After he'd rushed around the college putting up the posters, he wondered if he should go back to her office and return the drawing pins he hadn't used, and apologize for being so abrupt with her — but he really was pushed for time, as he'd said. He'd have to do it another day. He had an appointment and was already late. Then, later that evening he had to fly to Paris, because he had an important second job to do there.

He'd left the army, but they'd kept hold of him to work as an undercover agent for a government department which was currently protecting priceless art in the previously-occupied countries. Precious works were being unpacked from where they had been stored for safety during the war years, and being put back on display in museums — and, in some cases, given back to their owners.

Some of the art that had been stored was so valuable that it was vulnerable to being stolen by international criminals. He'd been warned that a gang in Paris was planning to steal some of it for private collectors, so he'd been asked to oversee the security arrangements of a major restoration operation taking place in the next few days. The authorities wanted those thieves caught.

Jon Hunter had been the man recommended for the job. He would be given military assistance — although they would leave it to him to say when he wanted help. They didn't want to break his cover. He had the difficult task of hiding his identity — juggling between being an investigator in a dangerous position, and executing his job as a council officer.

He was not an artist himself, neither had he much knowledge about the subject. Although he had liked much of what he had seen taken from the vaults where it had been kept safe from damage during the years of conflict.

Physically fit, Jon Hunter was able to fight, and was capable of defending himself if it became necessary. He owned and could use a firearm. That thought was constantly at the back of his mind, as he knew this task might become dangerous at any time. However, he also knew that this extra job of security work he had would only be temporary. When all the artworks were safely back in the galleries and collections they'd come from, his job would be over. He could then concentrate on what he liked doing best: looking after the environment, the countryside, parks and gardens. And encouraging all kinds of artists — musicians, painters and actors — to thrive.

He had also become genuinely interested in his work for the District Council. He genuinely wanted to promote the arts for the people in the town to enjoy. That was why he was putting up the notices around the college.

As he tramped around the campus putting up the posters, he thought it was a pity that spitfire of a secretary, Miss Crick, wasn't more amenable. She was an attractive girl — but obviously very proper. Nevertheless, she might be interesting to take out: she admitted she liked art, and he needed a girlfriend. But she ought to loosen up a bit!

* * *

So, weeks later, on the evening that the Art Exhibition had opened, Hazel remembered her first meeting with Mr. Jon Hunter, and the thought crossed her mind that he was getting back at her because they hadn't hit it off when they first met. She hadn't assisted him with putting up his posters — or was it more than the fact that, on first sight, they just hadn't liked each other?

Hazel knew an ex-army man like him would be used to giving orders. He was good-looking, but she decided that perhaps he just hadn't a kindly nature, which was a pity. Maybe that was why he wasn't married?

Devastated at the rejection of her painting, she was flitting down the wide hall stairs when she passed by a couple on the way up to the exhibition, and ignored their friendly greeting, 'Hello, Hazel. Going home already? The official opening isn't until seven o'clock.' She noticed the look of dismay on their faces as she brushed quickly by them without responding. Later, waiting at the stop for the bus home, she wondered whether she was adding to her misery by ignoring her friends.

'No use crying over spilt milk,' she told herself. Unfortunately, it gave her little comfort to remember she'd told so many people that she had painted a picture and they must be sure to go and see it exhibited. Now she'd have to face people asking her why they couldn't find her painting on display.

Eventually, off the bus and out into the evening light, Hazel kept her eyes fixed on the street pavement as she sped towards her parents' house. Although she had turned twenty, Hazel still lived with her mother and father because she was saving up for a home of her own.

Round the corner by the pub, and into the quiet street where her parents lived, Hazel took out her handkerchief, wiped away the tears that ran down her cheeks, and blew her nose. As her fingers struggled to find the front-door key, she knew her parents would be sympathetic, and didn't mind having to tell them the bad news.

She left her rejected picture in the hall and went into the sitting room. Her father, William Crick, was sitting in his armchair reading the newspaper. His eyes looked at Hazel over the top of the paper as she told him of her rejection.

'I'm sorry, love — just remember, you've got plenty of talent for art. Think about how many famous artists' work has been rejected in the past — like Van Gogh's was.' He gave a loud sigh and smiled sympathetically at his daughter, adding, 'Life is full of disappointments.'

Her mum called from the kitchen, 'Hello Hazel, you're home early. I'll dish up a meal for you in a minute or two.'

Hazel almost sobbed as she went into the kitchen and saw her mother at the hob, stirring the steaming vegetable pans.

'They didn't choose to put my picture up on display,' she said flatly.

Her mum dropped the wooden spoon, and with her head tilted on one side, showing her dismay, came over to her daughter and hugged her. 'Oh, love, I'm so sorry. Never mind, we'll put it up in the hall — it's a lovely picture.'

Later, in her bedroom, Hazel decided that she wouldn't give up painting, because she enjoyed doing it — but she wouldn't ever try and exhibit any of her work again.

The following day, having admitted to everyone that her painting wasn't in the Art Exhibition — and receiving both kindly comments and gentle teasing about her rejection — Hazel was able to forget her bitter disappointment and get on with her normal life. Until, that is, a month later, when Mr. Jon Hunter suddenly appeared in her office with the drawing pins he'd borrowed.

'Here you are, Miss Crick,' he said, rattling the box to show he hadn't used them all before plonking it down on her desk.

Distraught at having to face him, Hazel deliberately didn't look up from her work, and said in a flat voice, 'Thank you, Mr. Hunter.'

His chuckle annoyed her. So she added tartly: 'And, by the way, I must thank you too for refusing to hang my painting at the Art Exhibition.'

His head jerked around so that his eyes caught hers, as a puzzled expression creased his forehead.

Hazel continued, 'Now I suppose you feel even with me for not putting up your posters?'

'Miss Crick,' he said in a surprised voice, 'I don't know what you're talking about.'

'Oh yes, I think you do, Mr. Hunter!' With a shuddering breath, she added clearly, 'I'm sure you remember I didn't help you display the posters for the Art Exhibition as you wanted me to do — so out of spitefulness, you made sure that my painting was rejected.'

There was silence for a minute.

He drew in a long breath and regarded her severely before stating, 'Miss Crick, I had nothing to do with selecting the artwork to be exhibited.'

Hazel replied challengingly, 'No? Funny; I don't believe you! You organized the show, didn't you — you knew who would be on the selection committee, didn't you?'

Just at that moment, the principal, Mr. Payne, came into the office; and after adjusting his spectacles, he said, 'Oh, excuse me, Mr. Hunter. May I show this paperwork to Miss Crick? It will only take a few moments.' Coming up to his secretary, he started explaining some work he wanted Hazel to do.

Jon Hunter stood waiting for a couple of minutes, glancing at his wristwatch periodically and tapping his foot impatiently, then called out as he left the office, 'Sorry, I must go. I have to attend a meeting. I promise to see you after it's over, Miss Crick — and we can sort out your problem.'

He'd disappeared before Mr. Payne had finished giving Hazel instructions.

Her mind was in a whirl after the principal had also left her office, and she began to recall with regret what she'd said to Jon Hunter. She'd rudely accused him of having her artwork rejected! Had she any evidence he had done so? None! He'd certainly looked surprised — very surprised — and annoyed to be accused. He was a man of intense feelings — not the typical stiff-upper-lip-type Englishman. It shook her to think how passionate he might be.

She had attacked him — hit him hard with her words. How stupid of her to say what she had — even if she had thought it! Had she perhaps been harbouring resentment which she'd blamed on him, and it had just come out? She'd *presumed* he'd been the cause of her rejection.

He'd denied that he'd had anything to do with the selection process — and maybe that was right. *Oh, dear* — the sudden realization that she could have been mistaken made her want to weep.

Why had he had this strange effect on her, that she seemed to want to make an enemy of him? And yet she didn't really dislike him, did she? He fascinated her. In fact, to be honest with herself, she fancied him . . .

She ought to go and see him as soon as possible and apologize for her outburst.

He'd said he was going to a meeting, which Hazel knew was in the Conference Room at four o'clock and would be over at about five-thirty, just as she finished work. So that would be the best time to catch him.

As she was clearing her desk at the end of the day, she glanced out of the window and saw it had begun to rain. Fortunately, she kept a raincoat with a hood in her locker, and was able to slip it on.

It was pouring down as she left the college building and stood waiting in the car park by his car — she knew the big saloon he needed to carry all his work-related stuff, such as bulky piles of posters, art materials, musical instruments or theatre props. His name was on the badge notice displayed on the windscreen.

After looking around and seeing no sign of him, Hazel looked at her watch and sighed. She would miss the bus home if she kept waiting much longer. Although she had an umbrella, she was getting cold, and shivered. She looked around for somewhere to shelter. She huddled in a doorway, but it wasn't much protection from the rain beating on the concrete ground like a thousand drums and showering her. Every now and again, she rushed over to his car to make sure he hadn't come out of another door and was sitting ready to drive off.

She feared that if she went into the college hall to look for him, he might come out of the back door and she'd miss him. And, after all this inconvenience to try and speak to him, she didn't want to give up — besides, she really did need to apologize for her unreasonable, stupid outburst. Thinking about it, she wondered how she'd dared be so offensive to him.

When a gust of rainy wind almost swept her off her feet and her umbrella blew inside out, she grasped the car's back door handle — and found he'd left the vehicle unlocked. Perhaps she could wait in his car out of the rain?

The crack of thunder drowned the footsteps of someone behind her.

A hand smothered her mouth as she was savagely pulled backwards — a strong jerk that lifted her off her feet.

Before she could understand what was happening to her, she found her hands tied behind her, her ankles bound, and she was being lifted, helpless, into the boot of Mr. Hunter's car. As in a nightmare, her screams were unable to be heard, because the hand over her mouth had been replaced by wide parcel tape.

Vaguely aware that she'd had some kind of accident — no, someone had attacked her — Hazel struggled. However, finding that her bonds held her too firmly for her to free herself, and that she was locked in a dark chamber, she felt frightened out of her wits. She wondered if she was dead — but her pounding heart told her she was not.

She'd been abducted — bound and shoved into Mr. Hunter's car against her will.

A little later, when she sensed the car was moving, she fainted in panic.

2

Jon Hunter had no reason to look in the boot of his car as he dashed out of the college building and ran to his vehicle in the pouring rain. He shoved his briefcase onto the back seat before slipping into the front, mopping his wet face and hair with first his handkerchief, then with the cloth he kept in his car to wipe the windscreen. He cursed the wet English weather, hoping it would be better in France. He grimaced: that was, if he didn't miss the flight he was scheduled to take.

Jon was well aware he was running late. Important though his mission was — for him especially — he couldn't expect everyone taking part in the planned capture of the art thieves to be held up by him. It was too important an operation to abort. Valuable artwork would be spirited away to God knew where — probably to an acquisitive collector — and the general public would never be able to see it again.

On the other hand, he prided himself that he was the kingpin in this operation — would everyone else manage without him? He must do his best to get to Paris and set the sting up properly.

Starting the car engine, he became aware that a military police car was in the car park, waiting to escort him to the nearby RAF station where a plane would be waiting for him. He breathed a sigh of relief.

Half an hour later, he was waved through the military police gate, and drove onto the runway towards the waiting aircraft for his flight to Paris.

With the aircraft engines already started and making a racket, Jon swung his long legs out of the car and, standing, grabbed his briefcase and strode towards the aircraft steps, yelling to the waiting air stewardess: 'Get my suitcase from the boot of my car, will you?'

The stewardess immediately ran to

the car and opened the boot to retrieve his case. She gasped at what she found. Then, remembering she worked for military intelligence — where strange things occurred sometimes — she turned and shouted to Jon: 'Is the girl coming too, sir?'

Jon, halfway up the aircraft ladder, paused. 'Say that again,' he bellowed over the aircraft noise.

The air stewardess, carrying his suitcase, came nearer and asked loudly, 'Sir, there's a woman in the boot of your car. Is she coming with us?'

Jon frowned. Worried, he felt for the revolver under his jacket. Was this a joke — or some attempt to sabotage his coming operation?

His eyes immediately scanned the airfield for signs of any trouble. Nothing could be detected in the rainy autumn evening mistiness. He clambered quickly backwards down the aircraft steps and ran towards his car.

He gaped in surprised horror as he recognized Hazel, tied securely, lying in the boot of his car.

'What the hell are you doing here, Miss Crick?'

★ ★ ★

Determined not to freak out, thinking she was probably having a nightmare, Hazel's eyes looked pleadingly up at him. *Don't just stand there looking at me! Release me!*

He hauled her out of the car and ripped off the tape from her mouth — which made Hazel squeal — then he began to undo the straps binding her hands and feet.

Hazel felt herself in a daze as she rubbed her wrists and stamped her feet to get the circulation back — she *must* be having a nightmare! Yet, the cold wind was real enough — and certainly Mr. Hunter's fury was real enough, too.

'Who put you in my car?' he roared at her.

Still wobbly, Hazel held onto him tightly. Her long hair was flying around her head in the wind as her rain hood had fallen off. She tried to push some tresses from her face to be able to see Mr. Hunter's irate expression.

'We have to go, sir!' The air stewardess's urgent cry brought Hazel round to reality. This really was happening to her.

Steadying Hazel, Jon said angrily, 'I wasn't expecting this complication. Why on earth are you here?'

'I came to apologize . . . ' she said lamely, not daring to look up for long at his uncompromising expression, ' . . . for being so rude to you.'

He shouted, 'You must be crazy!'

'It's not my fault! I was waiting to speak to you after work at college . . . when someone hit me from behind. I was tied up and bundled into your car. I don't know who it was . . . or why they kidnapped me.' She shivered. 'I want to go home now.'

'Well, you can't, Miss Crick.'

'You can't stop me — '

His voice was quiet. 'Oh yes, I can.'

Stupefied, she kicked his leg so hard

he hopped further away from her.

The air stewardess tittered. Jon swung around and yelled at her, 'It's not funny!'

'No, it isn't, sir. Look, the pilot is beckoning to us urgently — we must get going.'

Jon Hunter's blazing eyes looked down on Hazel, enough to set her alight. Then he turned to the air stewardess. 'What are we going to do with her? There's no time to take her back to the guardhouse now.'

The woman shrugged.

Jon Hunter swore. 'She'll have to come with us to Paris. Get her handbag and let's put her on board quickly.'

If Hazel had been asked — or even had any choice about the matter — she would have declined the flight to France. But her protestations were ignored. 'No, no, please!' she cried. 'I don't want to go with you. I must get home.'

But she had no choice as she was firmly manhandled by Mr. Hunter — who was in no mood to argue.

Bustled up the aircraft steps, Hazel was half-pulled and half-pushed up until she found herself in the gloom of a service aircraft where there were no cosy seats. She was quickly strapped onto what looked like a school bench around the interior of the plane, with Mr. Hunter next to her.

This must be a nightmare, she told herself. *I'll wake up in a minute.*

But as the minutes went by, and the aircraft increased speed, she soon felt they were airborne.

Trying not to scream in terror, she bit her lip. Nevertheless, tears began to trickle down her face as her voice quivered. 'My parents will be worried about me . . . '

Mr. Hunter said, 'Cheer up, Miss Crick, we're only going to Paris — not Timbuctoo!'

Hazel tried her best not to sob, although her voice wobbled. 'I've never been abroad before. I haven't a passport — or any clothes or toothpaste with me . . . '

He sighed. 'There are a few shops in Paris, you know.'

Hazel rubbed her hands together nervously. Then she inhaled a deep shuddering breath. 'I can't afford anything . . . or the cost of a ticket back to England . . . '

'Relax, Miss Crick. I'll make sure you have some money. We'll phone your parents as soon as we arrive in France — which won't take long.'

'Mr. Hunter . . . what shall I do there? I'm scared!'

The stewardess had come towards them, carrying two cups of coffee. She'd heard part of their conversation, and said, 'I've got a few days' leave, sir. I'll look after her. She can stay at my hotel.'

'Thank you, Miss . . . ?'

'Marshall. Susan Marshall.'

'Thank you, Susan; I'm sure you'll make sure Hazel is well looked after.'

Hazel was dumbstruck at first to hear what was going to happen to her. There was apparently no going back to

England! But she still tried to argue. 'I can't speak French — I never was much good at French at school.'

Mr. Hunter turned to Susan. '*You* can, though, can't you?'

Susan smiled and nodded. 'Enough to get by, sir.'

'There you are. Miss Crick! You'll get free board and lodging for the weekend in Paris. You'll have two days to see the sights and shops — and probably a couple of nights on the town.'

Hazel almost dropped her cup of coffee as she felt him take her free hand and pat it. 'So, now you'll be all right, Miss Crick.'

'Don't keep calling me *Miss Crick*!' she blurted out.

'What would you like me to call you?' His soft voice in her ear and the warmth of his hand felt extraordinarily comforting.

'Hazel.'

'Mmm. A nice name! Now Hazel, you can look forward to a wonderful weekend — '

'But, Mr. Hunter, I don't want to go — '

'Then you shouldn't have been hanging about near my car, should you? I can only guess that you made the military police waiting to escort me nervous. Thinking you might be going to plant a car bomb, or something. And, as time was short for them to know what to do with you, they decided to put you out of action.'

Hazel touched her sore mouth gently with her fingers. 'They hurt me! They kidnapped me — it's illegal.'

'They were a little overzealous, I admit. I'll have to report them. I expect they are young lads and didn't know what to do with you. So they popped you into the boot of my car — very drastic, I know, but they would have released you later.'

'A comforting thought!'

'It wouldn't have happened if you hadn't been there, waiting near my car — making them suspicious.'

Hazel protested, 'I had to wait for

you, and it was raining. It was torrenting down!'

'Why was it so urgent for you to see me? I went back to your office after the meeting as I said I would — but you'd left . . . '

'I *did* wait for you, Mr. Hunter. I missed my bus home waiting for you . . . now I wish I hadn't bothered.'

'Hazel, if it was so important for you to see me, you should have waited longer. It makes me wonder why you were determined to speak to me. Were you hoping to have another go at me about your painting not being exhibited in the art show, eh?' He took a long breath in. 'Well, let me tell you that I asked a member of the selection committee why your work was not selected, and he explained that you had forgotten to attach the label with your name, the description of the work, and the price on it. They couldn't put it in the art show's catalogue, or hang it — or even contact you.'

Hazel gulped as the truth was

revealed to her. Her face crimsoned immediately. Yes, she remembered she *had* filled in the label — but, in her hurry to drop off the painting before going to work, she'd left the label in the drawer of her dressing table. How awful that she'd blamed someone else for her error!

Sickened with guilt, she said contritely, 'You are right, Mr. Hunter. I do remember now. I put the label in my dressing table drawer for safekeeping — I expect that's where it still is. I'm sorry I accused you of preventing my painting from being shown — it was unkind and thoughtless to have blamed you. I was very disappointed, that's all the excuse I have.'

He gave her hand a gentle squeeze. 'No matter. I'm glad we have agreed on why your picture was not on display, and that I was not to blame. I try not to let people down.'

Hazel murmured, 'I'm truly sorry, Mr. Hunter,' wondering what on earth he thought of her.

Mr. Hunter said cheerfully, 'Incidentally, I understand they thought your painting was very good, and they would have hung it had they been able to. Never mind; there'll be another art show next year.'

She felt his fingers stroke her hand again. It was like a mild electric shock, and it left her speechless. He continued: 'Anyway, you can enjoy the sights of Paris for a couple of days — and visit some art galleries. I think some holiday will do you good — yes, you need to shake off your rather staid attitude, and learn to enjoy yourself. I'm sure a few hours in Paris will open your eyes.'

'I'll make sure she does enjoy herself, sir,' chipped in Susan.

Hazel was staggered, hearing what Jon Hunter's opinion of her. He thought she was staid — at the age of twenty-four! But wasn't that the truth? Her parents were loving, but protective of their only child. Her childhood during the war years had been happy, but restricted as far as seeing anything beyond her town was concerned. But now she was being given the chance to see Paris — the home of painters — and he'd also mentioned that he'd been told she was a good artist after all!

Her sensible nature came to the fore. She'd got herself into this predicament, and she became determined to be positive and do what Mr. Hunter said: try and enjoy the experience.

How fortunate she was that Mr. Hunter was turning out to be such an understanding man. He could have her clapped her in a French prison — the Bastille, for instance, which she'd read in her history books was a terrible place. But no, he was offering her a paid-for weekend — she just hoped that was all. Paris, she'd heard, was not where people went for a quiet weekend; she was familiar with the paintings of Toulouse-Lautrec and his portrayal of the seedy city nightlife.

But, she thought, rather naughtily, *that might be fun!*

While Hazel was coming to terms

with her position, Jon was chatting to the air stewardess: taking out his wallet, he handed Susan a wad of notes. 'I'll get in touch with the British Embassy and have a temporary passport delivered to your hotel.'

'Thank you, sir. I've written the name of the hotel where we'll be staying on this piece of paper.' Susan handed him the information. 'Oh, look, the pilot has put on the landing light — we're coming in to land soon. Fasten your seatbelts, please.'

As Mr. Hunter sat beside her during the aircraft's descent, Hazel's mind fought with the knowledge that she was about to be thrust into an alien world. And also that this man was abandoning her. Never had she thought she would feel so bereft without him. She wondered when she would see him again — and whether he was as dependable as he'd told her . . .

Why was he going to Paris?

As soon as the aircraft came to a standstill, Mr. Hunter was up and grabbing his briefcase as if he hadn't a minute to spare. He bent over to whisper in her ear: 'Welcome to France.'

Outside, it was becoming dark, and there was nothing to see except some pinpricks of light.

Hazel couldn't say she was delighted to be there — she'd rather be at home. She felt like a piece of luggage as they escorted her out of the plane a little later and dumped her on an airfield that didn't look like a busy international airport. No, indeed — was it some kind of military base?

What were they doing here? Or, rather, what had Mr. Hunter come to this military base for? Why had he been treated like a VIP, taken by private aircraft to this godforsaken airfield?

She felt wary, convinced now that there was more to Mr. Hunter than she'd first assumed — he was hiding something. He'd rushed off the aircraft first, to be whisked away into a waiting American Jeep almost the very moment they landed, and only had time to call out, 'Enjoy yourselves, ladies. I'll be in touch as soon as I can.'

Once outside the plane, standing on the vast airfield, Hazel felt the cold blasts of air around her, and her thin-stocking-covered ankles felt they were turning into ice.

'Come on, Hazel,' Susan said in her ear. 'We won't have any transport laid on. We'll have to leg it to the control tower.'

'What is this place?' asked Hazel, still not able to make out any buildings in the gloom.

'It's a military airfield, near Paris. Come on, let's get going, Hazel. This wind is vicious. Airfields are always so bloody cold.'

It was difficult to converse as the girls battled to walk towards the control tower. Hazel felt she was suffering for her stupidity. If she hadn't jumped to the conclusion that Mr. Hunter was responsible for her painting being rejected, and then had the audacity to accuse him of being responsible for it, then she wouldn't be here now in a foreign county, in the biting wind, with no money — and no idea what was ahead of her.

'*Arrgh!*' She felt mad with herself, as well as about being tangled up with Mr. Hunter. And the vicious wind whipping her unprotected legs was an added punishment. But she had no alternative but to battle on as their destination became clearer.

The control tower was a simple concrete block with nothing but functional doors, windows, and an area where people were at machines controlling the aircraft. It wasn't busy, and Susan was able to find someone who showed her a phone she could use.

Competently, Susan spoke in French when she rang the exchange to find Hazel's home number in England. 'Hazel, come and speak to your mum,' she called, having seemingly had no difficulty getting through and talking to whoever answered the phone.

Now it was Hazel's turn to be responsible, to take the receiver and avoid sounding upset. She wanted to inform her mother than she was not coming home for a couple of nights, and reassure her that she was perfectly OK.

'I can't talk for long, Mum,' she explained. 'This friend of mine, Susan, suggested I went away with her for the weekend. So I thought it would be fun — and that you'd not mind.'

Her mother was full of questions — and objections. Why hadn't she mentioned it earlier? Who was this friend — was it someone she and Dad knew?

'Someone from work, Mum. No, perhaps I've not mentioned her to you — she hasn't been there long.'

'Yes, I know I didn't tell you. I didn't know myself that I'd be asked to go this afternoon. But the opportunity for a short holiday seemed too good to miss, although I had to decide on the spur of the moment. And I felt sure you and

Dad would agree that it's about time I spread my wings and saw a little more of the world.'

Hazel listened to her mother list all the difficulties she'd raised herself earlier. 'I can manage without my toothbrush and nightie . . . ' *Oh dear, no nightdress* — what *would* her mother think? She thought she'd better end this conversation before she said anything else that wasn't true.

'Mum, I can *borrow* a nightie — and everything else I need. I'll be fine — must go now — see you on Monday evening — give my love to Dad.'

Hazel rang off, knowing her mother was not altogether happy to learn about her suddenly flying the nest, and joined Susan, who was waiting for her. 'My mum's inclined to be a bit over-caring.'

'Most mothers are,' said Susan with a grin.

Hazel felt a little braver now that her parents knew she wouldn't be home until Monday. Apprehensive about what was going to happen to her — a bit excited, too — she asked, 'Are you sure you don't mind me coming with you?'

Susan shook her head. 'Of course I don't!' She began dialling a phone number, then asked in French for a taxi.

While they waited for their transport, Susan explained, 'I'm usually stranded by myself in cities in between flights, so it'll be nice for me to have company. Now, we may find the hotel hasn't a room for both of us, but we'll face that problem if it arises.'

Hazel hoped they wouldn't be split up . . . but she couldn't start complaining about anything that might occur — she'd put herself here in France, and would have to make the best of whatever happened to her.

The taxi driver chatted fast in French, obviously not realizing that Hazel couldn't understand most of what he said. But Hazel was occupied anyway, eagerly looking out of the window as the taxi sped out of the misty airfield and was she was soon able to see that she really was in France.

Soon she was amidst the sights, sounds and lights of the great city of Paris, absorbing glimpses of grand buildings as they whizzed by. She looked out of the taxi window in amazement — this was a life she'd never dreamt existed. French traffic seemed to her to be racing everywhere like bumper cars at a fairground — sounding their horns — chaotic! She didn't know how the drivers avoided crashes.

Evidence of the Nazi occupation of the city was being removed: buildings were being repainted and modern signs replaced the pre-war battered ones. Paris, she could see, was adopting a new spirit for the post-war era. It made her feel excited to be experiencing the clean-up taking place amidst the buildings of the enduringly age-old and esteemed city.

When the taxi eventually stopped and Susan paid the driver, Hazel clambered out onto the pavement, and was assaulted by the smell of French food and the sound of jazzy continental music as she stood surrounded by people in the bustle of a crowded street. Paris came alive at night — nothing like her home town of Highminster, which simply seemed to go to sleep then.

Susan tugged at her coat elbow and pointed at a very tall building nearby. 'Here's the hotel I usually stay at. We'll check in first, then go and find somewhere to have dinner.'

The tiny aproned lady in the little office at the entrance of the hotel, *la concierge*, recognized Susan, and chatted to her in French as she signed in.

Susan came back to where Hazel was standing, absorbed in all she was seeing. 'I'm afraid the only room available for both of us is right at the very top of the building — and there's no lift. This is a very old hotel and will probably be pulled down and rebuilt as many are now that the war is over.'

Yes indeed, the steps up to the top floor took a bit of climbing — winding around as if they were ascending a medieval clock tower. Hazel was glad she didn't have a heavy case to carry.

When they eventually made it to the very top landing and found the room, they saw that it was a dusty attic with two rusty beds. Hazel sniffed the dampness, and felt like saying, *I'm not sleeping here!*

But Susan didn't seem overly concerned. 'Well, this must be the worst room in the hotel — but we're only going to be in here to sleep. I don't fancy going around other hotels to find a better room — do you, Hazel?'

'Er, no.'

Hazel was just glad her mother couldn't see it.

The bathroom was out on the landing, and the plumbing rumbled and gurgled as Hazel had a quick wash and brush-up.

Downstairs and outside, they found a nearby café, and were seated and looking at the menu when suddenly Jon Hunter appeared and hailed them. He

49

was dressed casually, like the French men, and seemed delighted to have found them.

'Hello — don't order anything.' His long legs took him quickly up to their table. 'Let me treat you to a good restaurant, as this is Hazel's first visit to Paris.'

Before Hazel could protest that he'd done enough for her, considering her rudeness to him, Susan replied with enthusiasm. 'Thank you, Mr. Hunter; we would appreciate a good meal, our accommodation is somewhat basic.'

He looked serious. 'I can move you to a better hotel,' he offered.

'Well, thank you, sir . . . '

'My name is Jon.' He grinned. 'We're off-duty.'

Susan and Hazel had a brief discussion. Did they really want the bother of moving?

'Jon, Hazel and I decided to remain where we are. It's cheap, and central for sightseeing.'

Jon turned to Hazel and looked

deeply into her eyes. 'Are you sure?'

It seemed to Hazel that no matter what Susan thought, he wanted her to make up her own mind. She swallowed; his eyes were so attractive. She felt hypnotized by them, and a reply to his question seemed to stick in her throat. So, much as the offer of a better hotel room appealed to her, she nodded in agreement with Susan that they should stay where they were.

It was a short taxi drive to the restaurant Jon had chosen. It didn't look very special from the outside, but inside Hazel could see it had a cosy atmosphere a little like an English pub. She was thankful it wasn't the kind of place where you were supposed to dress up. She was dressed as she had been in the office all day, and most of the French women she noticed were elegant — even when still in their wartime clothes. However, Jon treated the ladies courteously, as if they were his friends or relatives. He let them choose where they wanted to sit, and pulled out their chairs for them so they could be seated. Hazel appreciated men with good manners.

After the waiter brought them the menu, Hazel stared at it, only recognizing the meanings of a few words.

Jon asked Hazel, 'Would you like snails, or frogs' legs?'

Shocked, Hazel felt like making a run for the exit.

Susan laughed as she picked up a menu. 'He's only teasing you, Hazel. Although I dare say they are on the menu, as they are French specialities. I'm sure we'll find something you'll like.'

It was comforting to have Jon there — he seemed at home, and spoke French fluently — but Hazel was a little in awe of him. Susan, on the other hand, was probably used to being taken out by senior officers, and so was more relaxed. She chatted happily, enjoying her aperitif, and Jon seemed content to listen to her.

Hazel wasn't used to drinking much. But she didn't feel left out because although she didn't know any of the people the banter was about, she was aware of Jon being polite to her. He was constantly looking at her as if, although she was not joining in the conversation, she was not being ignored.

She'd discovered he really was a caring man.

However, Hazel had a lot to look at, with people coming in and out of the restaurant, the view outside on the pavement, the foreign voices and laughter, the background music and aroma of the food being cooked. But she also noticed Jon seemed a little wary at times, and kept glancing around, making her wonder why that was. Did she imagine it? Was Jon expecting someone else to come and join them?

Or was he apprehensive that something was going to happen?

Hazel was hungry, and was soon enjoying the excellent French food — especially when a pleasant tiredness crept over her after drinking a glass of the delicious wine Jon had ordered. The thought of sleeping on the rusty bed in the attic didn't seem so bad now.

'I'm afraid I must leave you — I have to meet someone,' Jon said suddenly.

Hazel noticed his hurry to pay the bill and order a taxi for them.

As they waited for the taxi to arrive, Susan clutched Jon's arm. 'We could have walked back to our hotel,' she said, with a slurred, merry voice due to the several glasses of wine she'd enjoyed.

'Unaccompanied women are not safe out in Paris at night,' he said in stern tones that sounded as if he knew about possible dangers. 'Pickpockets and other rogues tend to come out after dark. Anyway, Hazel looks tired, and you can do your sightseeing when you are fresh in the morning.'

Hazel rose from her seat thinking he was right: she did feel very tired, and wouldn't appreciate having a long trudge back to their shabby hotel. 'Yes, I do feel absolutely whacked out. I'm not used to staying up late.' She immediately regretted saying that, as it seemed to reveal that she was a real country mouse.

She turned to look up at Jon and said, 'Thank you for forgiving me accusing you — thinking that you were responsible for my picture not being shown.'

His smiled was genuine. 'We all make mistakes. You must forget about it, Hazel. Think of going to the Louvre tomorrow, and seeing the feast of artwork there.'

She returned his smile saying, 'Thank you too for the delicious meal.'

He helped her on with her coat, saying, 'Your company has been a pleasure. There's your taxi waiting — I hope to see you tomorrow.'

He didn't say where or when he might meet them. Hazel had the idea he probably didn't know himself. She was curious to know what he was in Paris for.

As he didn't say where he was going, Susan — when seated in the taxi — remarked, 'I expect he's off to see a female for the rest of the night.'

Hazel didn't like to admit that Susan was probably right; he most likely had a date with some glamourous French lady, and she felt a pang of jealousy which stayed with her until they arrived back at their hotel. Why she should feel so possessive about a man she'd hated at the start of the day, she just couldn't understand. Strange, wasn't it? She certainly didn't mention it to Susan — who she soon realized, had enjoyed too much wine, and needed guiding and encouragement to be able to climb up the hundred or so winding steps to their attic room.

'I hope you've got the door key?' Hazel asked anxiously, after huffing and puffing up the last few steps, anxious to sit down in their room.

'Of course I have . . . somewhere . . .' Susan delved into her bag and her fingers rummaged around to find the key. In the end, not being able to locate it, she turned her handbag upside down and Hazel had to start picking up her things that fell out on the floor.

Susan was tittering, but Hazel didn't relish the idea of having to go all the way downstairs and having to ask the caretaker — in French — for a spare key. Then having to climb up all those stairs again!

'Susan,' she said crossly, 'what did you do with the key?'

Susan's face appeared a little startled. 'Sorry, Hazel. I really can't imagine where it is or what I did with it. I'll just sit down for a bit and think what I did with it, then it may come back to me.'

Or it may not, thought Hazel grimly.

This was a fine predicament. Susan was obviously slightly drunk, and didn't really seem to be worried about the missing key.

Remembering how Jon had not locked his car door, she tried the door handle, and to her amazement, found that the door swung open easily. Perhaps Susan had forgotten to lock it in their excitement about going out for the evening? They would have to look for the key in the morning.

'Up you get,' Hazel instructed Susan. She helped her get on her feet and, with her arm around her, guided her towards one of the beds and sat her down. From there, Susan needed no assistance to get herself into bed, and was fast asleep almost instantly.

But sleep didn't come so easily to Hazel. She didn't fancy huddling under the bedding that wasn't as pristine as she was used to. The pillow was lumpy and the quilt felt damp.

She went to the window and looked out over the streets of Paris, with lights twinkling and the faint sound of the traffic below. It had been a momentous upheaval to her life during the last six or seven hours. Some of it had been positively terrifying! Embarrassing, too, as she thought of how she'd verbally attacked Jon Hunter. And now she knew she inexplicably liked him, and felt indebted to him for his willingness to forgive her, but also for his generosity.

She'd once had a boyfriend who'd

played her along — until she discovered he was a man not to be trusted. He'd happily agreed to share expenses with her — she'd even lent him some money, but then she discovered he had no intention of ever giving it back. And, apart from spending her money, he'd been seeing another girl too. Consequently, her faith in men was not encouraging her to look for another.

But Jon Hunter was so different, wasn't he? He had shown her that he was thoughtful and dependable, the kind of man who would attract a girl to be his wife very soon. Although what did it matter to her if he was or wasn't the marrying type? Once they were back in England again she would probably see very little of him in the future.

Oh, well! She told herself it was nice to know he was here in Paris, and she would be seeing him . . .

Tiredness overtook her, and Hazel lay down on her bed. She must have dozed, for she thought she was only half-awake when she heard a click on the door handle. She was aware of some-one walking stealthily into the room.

But she could hear Susan snoring gently; and, thinking she must be dreaming after her eventful day, fell into a deep sleep.

3

Susan recovered quickly from overdoing her wine-drinking the night before. 'I'm used to getting up at set times,' she explained to Hazel, 'and having to be at the airfield to check in with the rest of the air crew.'

However, Hazel lay in her bed bleary-eyed, wondering where her mum was with her early-morning cup of tea. Then the reality of where she was came crashing down on her. Paris.

She was in Paris!

'We'll go to the café we went to yesterday — before Jon Hunter came and took us to the restaurant — we can get a nice cup of coffee and croissant before we start our shopping and sightseeing.' Susan sounded chirpy.

Hazel groaned.

'What's the matter?' asked Susan sharply.

'I'm feeling somewhat lost,' said Hazel; she was tired, felt unwashed, and had no clean clothes to wear. And she wanted a cup of tea — not coffee.

'Up you get, you can't waste precious time when we have so much to do,' Susan ordered. 'Go and have a shower. You can use my soap and toothpaste.'

Perhaps it was for the best that Susan was bossy, Hazel decided, or she would have languished in her bed all morning. Getting up, she saw the sun was shining, and the busy traffic could be heard outside, almost beckoning her to explore the city.

Later, refreshed and finding she was enjoying her French breakfast, Hazel hadn't a lot to say, but Susan was very chatty.

'I think we'll take the Underground — the Metro — I'll get some tickets that will enable us to travel all day to wherever we want. Now, we want a store that sells undies for you, and a pharmacy . . . '

When they were ready, they left the

café. While Susan gabbled on, Hazel was only half-listening, absorbing the atmosphere. And enjoying what she could see and smell — everything was so different from England. She wished she had a sketchbook with her, for many things she was seeing — simple things — would provide her with subjects to paint.

'Are you daydreaming about Jon Hunter?' Susan asked suddenly.

'N-no.' Hazel denied it, although he was not far away from her thoughts.

'He likes you, I can tell.'

'Don't keep on about it — I'm sure Mr. Hunter *doesn't* have a good opinion of me,' said Hazel emphatically. 'He's got every reason to be cross with me.'

Susan raised her eyebrows. 'Not any more. You may be surprised to know,' she said with a faint smile on her lips, 'he's given me a tidy sum to kit you out — '

'Ah, but I'll have to repay him.'

'Hazel! Jon Hunter doesn't strike me

as being short of a penny or two. He drives a Porsche in France — and his suits are tailor-made. Please don't worry about expenses. Let's enjoy ourselves. Explore the shops — the French make lovely things you can buy. And now the war is over, the luxury goods are increasing — I can't wait to get started looking — '

'But Susan, I want the cheapest stuff available. I only need some underwear and a toothbrush.'

'Heck, no! Your Mr. Hunter wants you out of your office clothes and looking as chic as the French women. You have a perfect figure, and there'll be plenty of clothes that will suit you. And as for the finishing touches, men like women to pamper themselves a little . . . indeed, it makes sense to realize that when a man takes a girl out, he is enhancing his image if she looks good. So forget wartime rationing and utility clothing, and look forward to seeing how the French women manage to attire themselves. And, as I've told you

64

before, he's given me plenty of francs for you to spend — by golly, I wish I was in your shoes!'

Hazel frowned as she scratched her eyebrow, realizing Susan was probably right for her not to worry about money, although she said, 'I expect he has many girlfriends to spend his cash on — not just a simple secretary like me.'

Much to Hazel's annoyance, Susan just tittered. 'I assure you, he doesn't think of you as just a simple secretary . . .'

Hazel blushed. Susan was older and more worldly-wise than she was, and men could seduce a girl — although she didn't think Jon Hunter would . . .

Susan interrupted her thoughts, saying, 'Anyway, I think we'll get the Metro now and start getting some things you need. So think about that, will you.'

Having left a tip for the long-aproned waiter, the girls headed for the Metro.

It was amazing for Hazel to see and take in where she was — all the sights and sounds that were so unfamiliar to her. Although she was beginning to get used to being in Paris, and everything didn't seem quite as strange the more she was there.

They found the things Hazel wanted without difficulty, and Susan encouraged her to take some money and shop for herself. Hazel tried not to be extravagant, still thinking she would have to repay Mr. Hunter for anything she bought — her house-buying hopes and savings were being spent at a fast rate.

But it was fun. The girls laughed a lot, and Hazel began to enjoy herself.

The next thing they did was to go back to their hotel so that Hazel could drop her shopping and didn't have to carry it around with her.

There was a note from Jon waiting for them. He asked them to meet him at the Palais de Louvre at two o'clock.

Having climbed up to their room to freshen themselves, they were ready to sally forth again.

As Susan locked their door, Hazel remarked, 'Last night when we arrived back here I couldn't find the key — and you were too boozy to know where it was. As it happened, the door wasn't locked anyway. So where did you put the key?'

Susan looked puzzled. 'I can't remember. Maybe the lady downstairs has it. Or the maid came in to change the towels and has left the key downstairs. But I haven't left anything of value in the room — have you?'

Hazel agreed she had few belongings left there, as they took their handbags with them, and as they had to hurry to meet Jon, they soon forgot about locking the door.

* * *

Jon Hunter felt restless as he waited for them at the Louvre. He had the responsibility of checking the progress of the workmen, who were in the dungeons, unwrapping the paintings that had been stored away during wartime. For him, it was a tedious job, and he would rather be engaged in the practical work than hanging around supervising and making sure none of the masterpieces came to any harm — or were stolen.

He knew some of the art thieves were ruthless. The worst kind of criminals that would kill for what they wanted. Woe betide anyone who got in their way. Being in danger himself, he had constant fear when he was around the precious artwork he was paid to protect.

Having Hazel and Susan to show around Paris was going to be some light relief for him. In fact, he was actually looking forward to seeing Hazel again. It surprised him that the little secretary had made such an impression on him. She had touched his heart because it was clear that she was not only pretty, but must be intelligent to hold down her important job as secretary to the principal of Highminster College. He had told her — somewhat cruelly, he now realized — that she was staid. It was probably true that she'd been brought up with old-fashioned parents, and that her childhood in rural England during the war had been somewhat restricted, with little opportunity for her to see the world.

But she was only in her early twenties, he guessed, and was about to learn and experience a wider view of life. And he felt keen to be able to give her the chance to expand her knowledge.

And, not to forget, of course, she was an artist. Therefore, having her come to the Louvre was his chance to allow her the best viewing of the magnificent works of art.

Ah, there they were — and, my goodness, how happy they looked chatting together. As he strolled towards them, his smile was generated by the pleasure he felt on seeing them.

But did Hazel look a little nervous? He hoped it was because she was in the grand palace of the Louvre, and not that she was intimidated at seeing him.

Susan naturally took over the conversation — she was used to being a good hostess — describing their shopping trip, and the fact that they hadn't had anything to eat or drink since breakfast.

'What would you like?' Jon deliberately asked Hazel.

'A cup of tea would be nice,' she replied.

Susan's laughter rang out as she put her arm around Hazel — and Jon felt envious that he couldn't. 'Hazel is not acclimatized to coffee or wine yet!' Then she added kindly, 'I dare say Jon will be able to find you a Coke, or a glass of lemonade, if you prefer?'

'Water will suit me,' Hazel stated quickly, as if not wishing to make herself a nuisance.

'Rain or tap water?' queried Jon, but with a lovely smile at her that made her realize he was teasing. She grinned, and he felt the sudden urge to place a peck on her cheek.

There was a restaurant at the museum, and after a light lunch, Jon began to escort the girls around some of the galleries.

While Hazel was deeply engrossed in what she saw, Susan was not as interested, and chatted to Jon — although he would have preferred to be viewing and sharing comments about the artwork with Hazel.

'Well, I think you've seen enough for one day,' he announced, just as Hazel thought so too.

'We certainly have,' said Susan — but Hazel caught his eye and smiled, saying, 'It's been wonderful for me seeing this art . . . ' She didn't seem to need to say any more to express her gratitude and the tremendous affect the art had had on her — but she was aware that Jon being with them had added to her pleasure.

He was obviously pleased to know Hazel had enjoyed herself.

'Your next engagement will be the cabaret at the Moulin Rouge,' he announced.

'It's hard to get tickets since the war,' Susan said.

Jon slipped his hand into his inside jacket pocket and withdrew some tickets. '*Voila!*' he said, winking at Hazel. 'Dinner and show for four — I'm bringing a friend.'

'Is he married?' asked Susan cheekily.

Jon didn't explain that he had deliberately asked a young unmarried man to entertain Susan so that it would give him the chance to be with Hazel — to get to know her better.

'I haven't any evening wear,' Hazel said.

'It's not necessary, just come as you are. There'll be other tourists there.'

As Jon was talking to Susan, making arrangements about the time they were to be fetched by taxi, Hazel noticed that a couple of men seemed to be waiting for him. She wondered why. And, as he said goodbye to her and Susan, the men rushed forward as if anxious to speak with him. He seemed to change from being a genial host to a man with an urgent job to do, as he hurried away. Hazel observed that the trio went not into another gallery, but to a small door in the panelling, not where visitors to the museum would normally go.

I wonder what Mr. Hunter is up to? There is something he is here in Paris for, that he is not telling us about. Mind you, I suppose there is no reason why he should — it's his business. But I'm curious.

Susan hadn't noticed, and Hazel didn't mention his disappearance into the wall of the museum as they went back to their hotel.

Paris was giving her a wonderful time — but the French didn't go in for afternoon tea, and Hazel missed it.

On their arrival back at their hotel, she soon had other more important things to concern her. Up near their front door was propped a package addressed to both of them.

'Ooh!' Susan gasped as she picked it up. 'I don't think we need wonder who this is from. It's got Jon Hunter written all over it.'

She threw the package to Hazel,

calling, 'Catch. It's for you. Open it.'

'Why me?' Hazel frowned; she sincerely hoped it did not contain more presents as she wondered how she would ever repay Mr. Hunter. Her savings for her own home would be decimated!

They sat on Hazel's bed to rest their feet after their long climb up the stairs.

'Look, it's from a well-known store. I bet he's used to ordering presents for his girlfriends. Let's see what he's chosen for us.'

The French store had wrapped things beautifully, and the two bottles of toilet water were very pretty. With a crunch of thin wrapping paper, they also found two packets of nylons and two gift boxes with the most delightful neck-laces inside. The necklaces were not the same, but both made the girls smile with pleasure.

'Oh, look — there's a little card.' Susan picked it up and read out:

'*To Susan and Hazel, to thank you for your company this weekend. You*

74

wouldn't let me pay for a better hotel for you — so I've sent you something else instead, and hope you approve. I'll pick you up at 7 — Jon.

'Approve? How could we not, Hazel? It's sweet of him!' she cried as she got off her bed. Going to the dressing-table mirror, she put on one necklace, lovingly stroking it. 'Which one would you like, Hazel?'

'I don't mind which one I have; they are both lovely.'

'Hey! We must watch the time. We've got to shower and get downstairs for when Jon and his friend arrive.'

The next half-hour was an exciting time, getting ready for their evening out.

What Hazel overlooked was that she hadn't remembered to mention again the mysterious disappearance and reappearance of the bedroom key the previous night. And the person that had floated by her bed, who might or might not have been a nightmare. In her hurry to beautify herself, there just didn't seem time to even think about such things.

She was aware, however, that she'd changed from being a scared mouse into Cinderella going to the ball — anyway, it seemed like that to her. Though she wouldn't go so far, she thought as she showered, as to think of Jon Hunter as her prince. Heavens, no! This was only a romantic evening out with him — and she intended to enjoy the experience.

'You'd better put plenty of the perfume on,' Susan told her, 'nightclubs tend to be hot and sweaty. Here, let me squirt some on the back of your neck and the inside of your forearms.'

Not having a sister, Hazel realized how much she had missed such girlish fun and chatter — but was enjoying it now.

Before long, they were trotting downstairs and there were their escorts waiting for them.

The men were not in evening wear (which Hazel did think was a pity, as she would have loved to see Jon Hunter in that — but then, she wasn't wearing an evening dress).

Introductions were made, and as Jon's ginger-haired, smiling friend Steve firmly took hold of Susan's arm and led her outside to the waiting cab, Jon offered Hazel his own arm, and gave her a wonderful smile. 'Come along, Hazel, let's have a good time.'

The dark streets were sparkling with light and full of people. The evening sights and sounds of the great city: a feast for the eye, and music to the ear. Especially when she was sitting so close to Jon, who was giving her a commentary on what buildings they were passing.

'Eighty-two, Boulevard de Clichy, home of the Moulin Rouge — look at the red windmill on the top of the building.'

Hazel tried to recall the pictures the famous French artist, Toulouse-Lautrec, had made in the heyday of the cabaret — colourful, lively dancers she'd seen pictured earlier that day at the Louvre. But, of course, those days were long gone, and now Paris was still recovering from its occupation. Nevertheless, there was an atmosphere in the building with the dancers and the famous traditional can-can music that was fun to see and hear.

When they had eaten and drunk — Jon had managed to find her a wine she liked — he asked her to dance. She felt a little apprehensive as she agreed. However, she discovered — as they moved in time to the music and chatted — that any awkwardness she'd had with him in the past had disappeared. He was a good dancer, and she felt happy in his arms.

Susan, she noticed, was quite happy with her partner too, talking away as she usually did.

The time seemed to fly in his arms. Hazel discovered, almost to her horror, that she didn't want to break away from him. She was shocked to realize she'd fallen in love with him.

And, when his lips gently brushed hers, she liked the feel of him and didn't want their embrace to end.

'You planned all this, didn't you?' she said, amusement showing on her face.

He chuckled. 'I thought perhaps I deserved a kiss?'

Hazel couldn't deny that he probably did — but did she want to start an affair with a powerful man like Jon Hunter? Although she knew little about him, she was sure he was in a different league to her, so she didn't answer.

'You don't like me?' He asked the question so seriously, as if he would be disappointed if she said *no*.

'Of course I . . . like you.' She almost said *love you*, by mistake — or was it a mistake?

He smiled down at her, almost relieved. 'That'll do for now,' he said.

'Honestly, I know so little about you, Jon. What are you doing here in Paris?'

'I have some business to attend to.'

'Shady stuff? I've noticed your connection with the military. The plane was waiting for you at the RAF airfield in England. And we didn't go to the airport when we arrived in Paris, we arrived at a French Air Force station. And even at the Louvre, you were escorted away through a private door . . .'

Jon laughed. 'You don't miss much, Miss Crick!'

She laughed with him. 'I'm not being nosey — it's your business, whatever it is. But naturally I'm wondering what you're up to — especially as we have become . . . friends.'

He stopped holding her, but held on to her hand, and pulled her gently to the side of the dance floor. 'Can you trust me?' he asked.

'That's a wide question, Jon.'

'My word, you *have* got your head screwed on — no, I am not suggesting you spend the night with me — '

Hazel joked, 'I don't think Susan would allow it!'

Jon nodded, with a grin. 'Probably not.'

Hazel looked up to read his face. No,

he didn't strike her as if he was going to try and persuade her to have an affair with him — and she was glad that he agreed he was just a friend.

She said, 'I do thank you, sincerely, for all you've done for me this weekend — I'll never forget it — '

'You could do something for me.'

'What's that, Jon?'

'Try not to concern yourself about what I'm doing in Paris. It's a job I've been asked to do — ordered to do — and I hope to complete it tomorrow. Then I'll return to England with you on Sunday evening, ready to start work on Monday morning.'

'It seems a bit strange for you to be working for Highminster Council,' Hazel remarked.

'I assure you, it's exactly what I want to do. I love nature, and want to spend my life protecting it. Looking after the environment and leisure pursuits, and enabling everyone to be able to enjoy them too. Don't you think that's a worthwhile occupation?'

'Indeed I do.' She twinkled her eyes at him. 'So, next time you need to put up some posters — leave it to me!'

'I hope I'm going to be able to see you more often than only in your college office?'

She laughed. She still didn't know what he was doing in Paris — he'd neatly avoided answering that question. She didn't even know where he was staying — but before she could continue her questioning, they were being interrupted by Susan and Steve walking towards them.

'Come on, you lovebirds,' said Steve, slapping Jon on the back. 'Let's have a drink before we leave.'

Susan looked as if she'd had enough to drink already, and Hazel thought that the quicker they left, the better — she might need some help getting her friend upstairs to bed!

Fortunately, the party ended without any more than high spirits. The men took the women home in a taxi, and practically carried a giggling Susan upstairs and placed her on her bed.

The fact that the room wasn't locked wasn't noticed by any of them, with all the laughter and effort they had to make in trying not to make too much noise and waken the other hotel guests.

Outside on the landing, while Steve was running down the stairs, Jon took Hazel in his arms again. 'Thank you for a lovely evening,' she whispered as he kissed her tenderly.

'To be continued,' he said, as he released her and dashed downstairs after Steve.

Even in the dull hall lights she saw Jon turn, look up at her bending over the banister, and blow her another kiss.

4

Susan wasn't as tipsy as Hazel feared she might be. But she was in a merry mood, and trying to talk to her about the missing key and someone crossing their room during the night didn't seem a good idea at this moment — the morning might be the best time to mention it, Hazel decided.

Still in an aura of a blissful feeling of being in love, and knowing the wall of mistrust between herself and Jon had crumbled a bit, Hazel didn't want to face anything more than to prepare for bed and crawl under the bedcover and sleep. One thing she was sure of was that her life had opened up to so many new experiences this weekend, and she would never again be exactly the same woman that had left England a day ago.

'Goodnight, Hazel,' called Susan from her bed. 'We must get a good night's sleep, because tomorrow we have to rise early if we are to do some essential sightseeing. My flight leaves in the late afternoon — I expect Mr. Hunter will arrange some transport to England for you.'

Sunday, thought Hazel, was certainly not going to be a day of rest. My goodness, she hadn't even seen the Eiffel Tower yet — or maybe she had . . . so many famous landmarks had been pointed out to her as they drove through Paris.

★ ★ ★

Waking when Susan's alarm clock sounded was painful. Despite her bed being creaky and the mattress lumpy, Hazel had slept very well.

Immediately, the girls had to wash, dress and pack their things.

'We'll leave our bags here until we collect them later,' said Susan; and as usual, Hazel was content to allow her to make the plans — Susan was so good at it, being used to spending a few days at a time in cities around the world.

Hazel hadn't much to pack, and while she was waiting for Susan in the bathroom, she sat on her bed — and noticed her wardrobe door ajar.

That's funny — I don't remember opening that, or putting anything in it.

Rising, she went towards the wardrobe and, opening the door a little more, peered in.

It was dark inside.

Walking over to borrow Susan's torch, Hazel took it and shone it inside the wardrobe. The space inside was enough for her to notice it was quite roomy, and there appeared to be another small door at the back that looked as if it would open. She stepped inside to examine it.

It was musty, and Hazel hoped she would not come face to face with a big spider.

Pushing to open the small door, there was a bit of resistance and a squeaky noise. But that didn't dampen Hazel's curiosity. Easing the door open some more, she shone the torch ahead of her, and saw what looked like an attic room ahead. Curious, she went further in, and saw she was in a storeroom. Above her, a skylight provided light, and on the floor underneath were some cloths covering a variety of boxes.

Hazel stood contemplating them, thinking they might be spare bedclothes that might have been stored there. Bending down, she flicked one of the covers back — and almost screamed. Because what she saw was a pile of guns!

They were not the kind of guns hunters treasured, kept in specially-designed cases and used for shooting exhibitions or competitions. Hazel thought they looked old, well-used, and the kind of rifles military men might use.

Jumbled in her mind was the remembrance of someone crossing their bedroom during the night time. So, it was true — she hadn't imagined it — she *had* seen a figure in their bedroom last night, and the previous night when she couldn't sleep.

Who was that man who tiptoed by her bed at midnight, and why did he store guns in this hiding place?

Shaking a little from her frightening discovery, Hazel became aware of Susan calling her back in the bedroom. But by the time she had collected her wits, and scrabbled out of the wardrobe room and through into the bedroom, she found that Susan had gone!

Eek!

Hazel ran through the bedroom towards the landing, shouting, 'Susan, I'm here! Where are you?'

Alas, she was too late to catch quick-footed Susan, who'd obviously thought Hazel had already left the hotel and had run after her.

All alone — now what was she going to do?

She noticed Susan had left her bag on her bed — so at least Susan had planned to return to collect it later, as she had said she would. However, that might be a long time — precious time when Hazel could be out seeing the wonderful sights of Paris.

Hazel dumped herself down on her bed and almost cried with frustration. Then she decided that Susan had probably just gone around the corner to the little café where they had had their morning coffee and croissant. She would join her there.

Leaving her bag of belongings behind too, Hazel slipped on her raincoat, as the day seemed cooler than it had been the day before — and purple clouds visible from the bedroom window suggested rain coming. Grabbing her handbag, she tore down the stairs to ask the old woman caretaker — in broken French accompanied by gestures — if she had a message, or even knew where Susan had gone.

But after trying her best to make herself understood, Hazel had to give up. She couldn't make the old lady understand. So she smiled at the caretaker, thanked her, and then dashed out of the hotel.

Out in the street, Hazel tried to

remember where the café was. And she felt quite proud of herself when she found it. Looking anxiously around, she searched for a sight of Susan — but no luck: her friend wasn't in the café, nor outside at the pavement chairs and tables.

Thirsty, Hazel sank down on a café chair, and when the waiter came she was able to indicate that she would like a coffee. She knew she had a little French money, but had no idea how many francs Susan had given her. Scrutinizing the menu, she looked at the prices of the food on sale, and worked out roughly how much she had.

The coffee was delicious, and it gave her a sense of well-being to start the day.

But what shall I do?

Susan had vanished. Maybe she had a bit of a hangover from last night's copious wine she'd drunk, and was now at a chemist looking for some medicine to cure it. But Hazel couldn't wait around for hours, not when she had the opportunity to explore this beautiful city.

After half an hour, she scribbled a note for Susan and left it with the waiter, with her payment for the coffee and a tip — which, she'd noticed, the French waiters expected.

Over the road was a newspaper kiosk, and she made towards it — dodging the traffic and ignoring the blaring horns. She bought a small Paris guide with some useful French words and phrases.

She decided to go to the Louvre, find Jon Hunter, and tell him what had happened. Although he hadn't told her so, she felt sure he was working there — or they might know where he was. Or Susan might have contacted him.

Being young and fit, Hazel judged that, with the help of the little map she'd acquired, she could walk there. My goodness, how big the boulevards and buildings were! Elegant tree-lined walkways, with families strolling about on a Sunday morning, were a treat to see.

The weather was changing as she walked; the bright early morning sun became clouded over and rain threatened. Although she became hot with the exertion of pounding the pavements, she was pleased she was wearing her old raincoat. Her office shoes were well up to a long walk too.

When Hazel arrived at the palace museum, she was worn out and anticipated being greeted warmly by Jon — and able to have a drink.

But no such luck.

Her French was not sufficient to make herself properly understood. The officials she tried to ask about the Englishman Jon Hunter obviously didn't know him. They shrugged their shoulders in the Gallic fashion.

It was so disappointing to be in the Louvre, with all the art treasures there she would have loved to see, and yet know she must leave.

After finding a café, and buying a very expensive lemonade, Hazel realized she had no option but to make her way back to the hotel and hope Susan was there.

Looking at her watch, she was alarmed to find the time had sped past. She decided she must be brave and take the Metro — she couldn't possibly walk back to the hotel, for it would take far too long.

Aware that Susan had to go to the airfield in the afternoon to check in with her flight crew, Hazel realized she might miss her if she didn't get a move on. Gulping the last of her drink, she took out her little map and searched for the nearest Underground station.

★ ★ ★

'Hello, hello, is that Mr. Hunter?'

The woman sounded frantic, and Jon deliberately answered with a clear, calm voice. 'Speaking,' he said.

He heard the intake of breath before Susan wailed, 'Hazel has gone, Mr. Hunter.'

'What do you mean, *gone* — is she ill?'

'No, she's vanished.'

Jon became stern. 'Susan, have you been drinking?'

'No, I haven't! I've been looking all around Paris for Hazel.'

Jon was irritated. He could well do without this interruption to his work. Things were becoming critical for him to start to pounce on the wrongdoers, and having to sort out the women's problems was nothing but an inconvenience he could well do without.

'Now look here, Susan. You know I have an important mission this morning, and it's about to commence. I don't want to be disturbed right now — give me an hour or two to finish this operation, and I'll be glad to assist you in any way I can.'

'Sir, please remember *I* have a flight to check in for this afternoon.'

His exasperation was audible. 'All right, Susan. Let me know the moment you find her.'

He put the phone receiver down with a clatter, muttering, 'Women! They're nothing but trouble . . . and Hazel has caused me more than enough already.'

The phone rang again immediately. Susan sounded anxious. 'Mr. Hunter, you've got to help me, *now*!'

With a long, pained sigh, Jon answered. 'OK. What do you want me to do?'

'Find her.'

'Why can't you?'

'Mr. Hunter, I've spent all morning looking everywhere for her — and I haven't a clue where she is. All I can tell you is that she did go to the local café for breakfast this morning — the waiter told me. He noticed she crossed the road to the kiosk on the corner, and upon enquiring, I was told she bought a map of Paris.' Susan took a deep breath and continued, 'And she left her bag at the hotel, so I presume she intends to come back here — only I have to leave to catch my flight soon.'

Jon frowned. Susan's story did sound credible. Her voice was unsteady, as if she was truly upset.

'All right, I'll come round,' he said reluctantly.

Jon was struggling not to show his fury after receiving this phone call from Susan and learning she had lost Hazel. And had no clue as to where she was.

He stood looming over the air stewardess. 'What do you mean, she ran off without saying anything to you?'

'That's the way it was, sir. I was in the bathroom, and when I came out she'd gone. No message or anything.'

Jon swore silently.

Susan looked and sounded genuinely upset. 'I'm sorry — I can't think why she's hopped it. *La concierge* downstairs in her office told me she saw her go out, and that before she left the hotel, Hazel had tried to tell her something — but she couldn't understand what it was.'

Susan's frown showed she was puzzled as she continued, 'I went outside to look around for her. She wasn't at the café where we have our morning coffee. I can't think where she could be.'

Jon was dismayed to hear that Hazel had taken it into her head to lead him a dance by going missing — on the day they were to return to England, too — and now his mission was in jeopardy.

Jon's anger boiled. Weeks of work had been put into preparing to catch the thieves who he knew planned to steal six valuable miniature paintings that came from a private house in Provence. They'd been stored away during the war years in the Louvre cellars for safekeeping, and today he was hoping to arrest the criminals and return the paintings to the owner.

The operation would have to be cancelled, because his first responsibility was to find Hazel. He wouldn't have the time to do both. He would never feel happy until he found that wretched woman — nor able to concentrate totally on the mission — because he'd promised her parents that he'd look after her.

He gave an abject sigh. She just *would* play up at this crucial time for him.

He deeply regretted that he would be

unable to prevent the thieves from spiriting the paintings away — they were small and easily concealed, and he'd heard how they intended to do it. By tomorrow, they would be abroad, and would most likely land up in an art collector's hoard. And the thieves would be free to steal more artwork.

Damn! All that hard work for nothing!

He wondered where on earth Hazel could be. What had got into her? Didn't she realize how dangerous it could be for a young woman to be wandering the streets alone? Especially as it would be getting dark soon. Not that he thought that Hazel was a flighty type of girl, or that she hadn't much common sense — she had. That was the puzzling thing.

And he had one other reason to be worried — he'd become fond of Hazel Crick. *Very* fond of her — but it didn't stop him from feeling angry with her too. So it wasn't difficult for him to accept where his duty lay. Hazel came first.

He'd have to tell Susan to go ahead and check in with the rest of her cabin crew in a couple of hours, and leave Paris. Hazel was his problem — not hers.

He had no doubt that Susan had been a great companion for Hazel. He could tell they'd become friends. Consequently, he didn't think Hazel would play a trick on Susan, rushing off somewhere deliberately and causing her companion distress.

Susan had told him that after looking for Hazel, she'd gone back to her hotel and found that her friend had left her bag there — as if she intended to go back and collect it.

Her behaviour mystified him. Hazel hadn't enough money to go back to England. He could always ring the British Embassy; but perhaps, before he started a hue and cry for her, he should take a look around himself.

He prayed she hadn't had an accident ... But before he rang the hospitals, he must search the girl's hotel himself. Gloomily, he looked out of the window at the darkening sky. Raindrops were beginning to run down the window.

Oh, Hazel; I thought you cared for me last night — why have you done this to me?

★   ★   ★

Hazel was almost in despair when she entered the Metro and looked at the long list of stations. Fortunately, she recognized the name of the station where she had to go. This gave her courage to go to the ticket office a get a ticket as she only had to say the name of the station. The cost almost depleted all her cash, but she felt sure that once she arrived at her destination, she would be somewhere near the hotel and would recognize the area — she certainly hoped so.

She tried her best not to look as if she was as scared as she felt. Fortunately, the other passengers hardly noticed her — at least, so she thought, until a muscly man in a beret kept looking at her and got up out of his seat to come and sit by her. Too close.

Forcing herself to breathe normally, Hazel looked anxiously out of the window as the train arrived at each station.

When she saw the name of the station she was looking for, she leapt up and made for the train doors; but, as she was the only passenger in that carriage to disembark, she was aware that the man who had come to sit by her was now following her. Was he an undesirable who'd noticed she was a young woman alone and looked vulnerable?

With a thumping heart, Hazel fought her panic and walked quickly towards the exit.

'Hazel!'

She heard her name called and stopped, petrified. How did that man know her name?

5

Hazel felt trapped as she heard pounding feet behind her, running up fast. Breathing raggedly, she shuddered and shut her eyes tight — fearing the worst. Grabbed by a steely hand over her arm, preventing her from escaping, she gave a anguished cry.

'Hazel! Are you all right?'

The English voice made her open her eyes to find ginger-haired Steve looking down at her with a concerned look on his freckled face. 'Sorry to frighten you, Hazel,' he puffed, out of breath from running after her.

Swallowing with relief to see a face she knew, Hazel wiped away the tears that had begun to form in her eyes.

'Where have you been? We've been looking all over Paris for you.'

Too overcome — too relieved — to speak, Hazel gulped back the tears that had started running down her cheeks.

'I . . . I'm sorry,' she said. Trying to control herself, she began to explain what had happened to her and why she had gone to the Louvre looking for Jon Hunter. But her words sounded inadequate for a good explanation.

'Never mind telling me what happened now,' Steve said kindly, producing a large men's handkerchief for her to dab away her tears. He took her elbow and gently steered her towards the ticket barrier.

Once outside the station, Steve went to the nearest telephone booth and put her inside before he picked up the receiver and dialled a number.

'Jon,' he said joyfully, 'I've found Hazel.'

She couldn't hear what Jon said, just Steve's words: *frightened, crying, upset, at the Metro phoning you*. It was a good description of how she felt. She was anguished to hear Steve telling Mr. Hunter about her distress. What an idiot he must think she was to have got herself in that state!

After assuring Jon that Hazel appeared to be all right, Steve listened for a minute and then rang off.

'Hazel,' he told her, 'Jon will be here in a few minutes. Let's go and sit in the station waiting room and wait for him.'

Hazel was still suffering too much from the effects of the day's experience to be able to offer any coherent explanation for her absence; and when she tried, Steve told her to wait until Jon arrived.

It wasn't long before the familiar figure of Jon Hunter marched into the station lobby; looking around, he soon spotted his quarry.

He didn't say anything to Hazel, just nodded at her with pursed lips and looked at her with an exasperated expression.

'Thanks, Steve. Go and tell Susan she may go to the airfield to join her crew now,' he said in his commanding-officer voice.

Steve left them immediately.

Jon plonked himself down on the bench where Steve had been sitting with her. 'So, Hazel, what have you got to say for yourself?'

Hazel, who had realized she'd caused trouble, only whispered, 'I'm sorry.' But her tears spoke for her.

'Now, now, Hazel.' Jon suddenly became less authoritarian and placed his hand around her shoulders, saying, 'Let's go somewhere we can talk quietly, and you can tell me what you've been up to. Have you eaten?'

'I've only had a coffee and a lemonade all day — '

'Dear me, we'll have to do something about that.'

It was so comforting to be with him. He didn't attempt to make her rush, nor did he seem want to inflict any more distress on her.

Guiding her to the nearest restaurant, he stopped and looked at the menu outside. 'This looks as if it will provide us with a meal. It's early — there will probably be very few diners here.'

In fact, after they'd walked in, they

found they had the place to themselves.

Choosing a corner table, Jon pulled out a chair for Hazel, sat her down and beckoned to the hovering waiter.

'They may say they are not serving meals for another hour — but I'll ask what they can provide for us.'

Hazel sat back in her chair. She felt exhausted, but so relieved that she was with Jon. She listened to his now-familiar mellow voice that sounded so reassuring. She studied his clear blue eyes and watched his mouth — so kissable — as he chatted to the waiter, and knew he had captured her heart. Only she feared he would not have a good opinion of her now.

Most likely he was just being kind and understanding as he could see she'd been distressed — and still was. Doubtless, in his opinion, she'd shown what a silly, unreliable woman she was. Not the kind of woman he'd choose to befriend, let alone marry. She'd seen enough of him now to know he was a very capable and worthy man, and he probably had a girlfriend or two — with his looks, surely he already had an army of women who had claims on him.

'*Du pain, du beurre, un potage . . .*'

Hazel recognized the French words for bread, butter and soup. Jon turned to her and asked, 'The cook can offer us a dish of fish or veal or underdone beefsteak — which would you like?'

Her mind had trouble to think of what he was asking. 'I don't mind,' she said weakly. Then, seeing the frown appear on his face, she pulled herself together and said, 'Fish, please.' She certainly didn't fancy anything under-done — but then, she wasn't surprised that Jon ordered it for himself.

A glass of mineral water appeared in front of her, and also a beer for Jon.

'Will you excuse me? I want to ring Steve and tell him where I am. Won't be long — don't go wandering, off will you?'

She had to smile . . . sadly. From now on, he was going to treat her like a naughty child.

By the time he returned, a serviette and a bowl of steaming soup with a wonderful smell had been placed before her.

She couldn't resist tasting the soup and, finding it delicious, was tucking in when Jon approached the table. His face was set in a long-suffering expression. He sat down, saying, 'Steve is coming to join us. Susan is on the way to the airport, and Steve reckons she won't be late and get into trouble.'

Taking a much-needed sip of water, Hazel said, 'I am very sorry to have caused you all so much trouble. You must think I'm an idiot.'

'No, I'm sure you had a good reason for doing what you did. Get that hot soup finished first — then you can begin to tell me what happened.'

He ignored her efforts to talk and, picking up his beer glass, began to relish his drink. Then he took out a notebook from his inside jacket pocket and scribbled a note.

Steve came into the restaurant with a

face almost as red as his hair.

Jon regarded him with a grin. 'Said goodbye to Susan, eh?'

Steve grinned. 'Yes. She's on her way. May I join you?'

'Do. We've already ordered a meal. Here's *le menu*.'

Steve sat, but before he picked up the menu he turned to Hazel and said, 'Susan is sorry not to have seen you, but is glad you are safe. She was most upset to have missed you and will be in touch.'

Hazel put down her soup spoon. 'I'm so sorry . . .'

Jon thumped his hand on the table, saying, 'Don't start all that sorry business again, Hazel. We know you'll have an explanation for your behaviour. Let's have our meal in peace first.'

He could be so domineering.

Hazel did as she was told, and continued finishing her soup.

Steve remarked, 'I could eat a horse.'

'Shh! Don't say that! Hazel may think you are going to — they eat horse meat in France.'

Steve looked at Hazel ruefully, but she pretended not to notice.

The food, when it came, was good, and all three enjoyed their meal: saying little, but making odd comments.

Relaxing with a coffee and liqueur, Hazel felt rested and ready to tell them what had happened to her — but Steve interrupted her thoughts by looking at his watch and saying, 'Sir, it's not too late to go after those crooks.'

Jon also looked at his watch, then shook his head regretfully. 'Nope,' he said, 'I've got a young lady here to look after.'

Hazel's ears had pricked up. Crooks? She'd suspected, hadn't she, a long time ago? Jon was involved in some military affair: he hadn't just come to Paris for a joyride. So she wasn't too surprised to hear the men had some sort of official operation planned.

But then, Jon said he had to look after her, and therefore couldn't do it.

Guilt hit her. No way did she want to

be a nuisance and prevent them from doing what they wanted or they were supposed to do. She said, 'Oh, don't bother about me. I can wait for you to do whatever you have to do.'

The pained expression on Jon's face embarrassed her. He took a gulp of his drink, and stared up at the ceiling as if he was thinking deeply. And sighed. He turned to her and said, 'Hazel, you don't understand what we had planned to do today.'

Did he really think she was a foolish woman — not reliable enough to be told about his mission? She said, 'I know you think I'm not to be trusted — but you could chain me to some railings if you like, so I'll be there when you get back.'

Steve guffawed, and even Jon smiled. He leant forward and patted her hand. 'You've been through enough for one day.'

Hazel bristled. 'I'm fine. I want you to do whatever you've planned. I hate to think I've caused you to abandon it.'

Jon scratched his eyebrow. 'Hmm. Alas, it's too late now.'

Steve said, 'I think we should try, sir . . . after all the trouble we've been through to make sure the sting will work. Hazel can come with us — it won't make any difference.'

Jon was deep in thought.

He glanced at his watch again. He spoke slowly, as if considering. 'I suppose we are all right time-wise if we hurry. But we've not brought those small packages we prepared and need to put the little paintings in.'

Steve tapped his arm and pointed out of the window. 'Look, there's a *tabac* shop over the road, I can see it. We could buy some cigarette packets — they'd work.'

Jon stood up and looked outside. 'I suppose they might . . . '

Then he sat down again and commented in a deflated voice, 'Anyway, we haven't any ammunition. I have my firearm, but that's not enough if there are several armed men to arrest.'

Hazel's eyes widened in amazement, hearing them talking about having to arrest armed men — and having no guns to do the job. Suddenly recollecting what she'd found that morning, she blurted out, 'I know where there are some guns — at least, rifles, I think they are. Masses of them.'

Both men looked at Hazel in astonishment.

Hazel blinked as she was stared at. 'I discovered some early this morning — '

Jon found his voice first, and in a sharp tone enquired, 'What the hell are you talking about — finding some guns — where?'

Hazel gulped. He could sound so harsh. His officer-style commands were so frightening — no wonder soldiers did as they were told, she thought. But she wasn't one of his soldiers. 'They may not be any use,' she replied, deliberately casually, and took a sip of her coffee.

'They won't be if you saw them in a shop window!' Steve said.

'This is not a game we are playing!' retorted Jon.

Hazel put down her coffee cup with a clatter, and did her best to stare up at his frowning expression. 'I never suggested it was a *game*, Jon!' She gave another gulp as his eyes bored into her. 'I merely told you that I found an arsenal of guns this morning. I don't know who they belong to — or even if they work. I don't know anything about guns.'

Jon relented, and asked her more politely, 'I'm sorry, Hazel, if I appear to be desperate. You can't be expected to know what is at stake. I can only assure you that catching thieves is why I came to Paris. And for me, personally, it is not only the paintings which are only valuable objects I try to protect. There is the human side of theft. People are *hurt* by theft.'

Hazel noticed he was speaking from his heart, and marvelled at his sensitivity to people's feelings. She swallowed. He was being serious — and his work was not just for his own gain or glory. And she admired him for that.

'This morning,' she began, 'I — '

He interrupted her. 'Now — quickly, please — can you tell me where you found these guns, so that I can at least take a look at them?'

'At my hotel, up in the attic bedroom where Susan and I spent the night.'

Steve butted in, 'Susan didn't tell me anything about them.'

Hazel replied curtly, 'Susan didn't know. After I found them, I went to tell her, but she'd gone. That's why — '

'Are they still there?'

'How should I know?'

Jon drummed his fingers on the table. 'Do you *think* they may still be there, Hazel?'

'Well, I can't say. To me, it seemed as if they had been stored there for years. I had the feeling — I thought it was a nightmare — that someone had entered our bedroom during the night. Perhaps they needed to get to that storeroom, but I was too far asleep to know for sure. Anyway, it was a bit scary.'

'Why didn't you tell Susan?'

'I told you, after I'd discovered the store of guns and wanted to tell her about it, Susan had already left the hotel. We were looking for each other — '

'Why didn't she wait for you?'

'Because she didn't know I was in the wardrobe cupboard, and I had found the door at the back that led into another area where the guns were hidden. She must have thought I'd gone for a coffee at the café round the corner and went to look for me. Somehow we missed each other . . . '

'Hmm.'

'Are you sure you didn't dream all this?'

'I didn't dream about the guns — that, I'm sure of.'

'So, if we went back to the hotel, you think they would still be there?'

Hazel's mouth twisted as she thought about it. 'All I can say is that there were far too many guns for one man to carry off.'

Steve said, 'Perhaps we should take a look, sir?'

Jon appeared to have made up his mind quickly. 'Right. We'll give it a try.'

Turning to Steve, he instructed, 'Go and buy a dozen large-sized packets of cigarettes. Take them to our planned exchange point. We must make sure that the paintings have been stolen before we can arrest the robbers . . .'

Jon took a deep breath and went on: 'Then meet us at the hotel — upstairs, where Hazel said the guns are hidden — and don't take long about it.' He took out his wallet and gave Steve some money.

Steve shot out of the restaurant while Jon called the waiter and paid the bill.

'Come with me,' Jon ordered her when they were on the pavement walking towards her hotel.

Hazel felt like a dog at his heels. She felt angry that he hadn't given her time to explain exactly how she came to find the weapons. He was treating her as if she was someone he had to drag along with him, and his long legs made her trot to keep up with him.

Fortunately, having rested and eaten, she felt refreshed, and was glad she was wearing her flat office shoes.

Rounding the corner before they came to the entrance of the hotel, he stopped abruptly. 'I think it would be better if I keep out of sight. You go in and chat with the old lady at the desk — I'll slip by and go upstairs while you're talking to her.'

'Cripes! What can I say? My French isn't up to holding a conversation — '

He looked down at her coldly. 'You got us into this mess, Miss Crick. Now you can help us to get out of it. You've got a phrasebook — use it. Make sure you have the room key, in case Susan handed it in.'

She could have kicked him. But he'd already walked off and was soon waiting just outside the entrance to the hotel. As the job he wanted to do sounded official, she thought it wasn't the time to be quarrelling with him. No, indeed; now was the time to show her grit and determination to assist the man she loved to get on with his mission — which sounded very important.

Walking by him as if she didn't know him, Hazel fished the phrasebook out of her handbag and went into the hotel lobby. She walked up to the glass and was relieved to find the little French caretaker in the porter's office.

Hazel tapped gently on the window to attract the woman's attention.

'Excusez-moi, Madame.'

Seeing her, the French woman smiled and, going to the key rack, took down a key and handed it to Hazel. Hazel was delighted she wasn't expected to talk, and was just turning to go, when she was summoned by the caretaker and given a letter. A quick look at it, and she realized the letter was from Susan.

'Thank you,' she said, accepting it. 'Merci, madame.'

Glad she didn't have to say anything more in French, Hazel moved away towards the stairs and looked up, wondering if Jon was already up at the top. But to give him more time, she opened the envelope she'd been given, to read the letter. It had obviously been written in great haste:

Dear Hazel,

So pleased to know you are found — it was such a shame we missed each other and were not able to go sightseeing together today.

It was tremendous fun being with you in Paris, and I hope you'll keep in touch.

Must rush now to check in for my flight!

Susan

At the bottom of this missive was an English address and phone number, so Hazel knew Susan wanted her to continue being her friend, and felt delighted she did.

The urgency of her present situation crashed down on her. She shoved Susan's letter in her bag and, taking a quick look around to make sure Jon was not hiding anywhere downstairs, she braced herself and began to climb the stairs — hoping that this would be the last time she would have to do it. Especially as Susan had left already, and she really didn't fancy spending another night up there alone.

Puffing from the exertion of climbing as fast as she could, Hazel managed to reach the top landing to see Jon standing outside her bedroom door. 'You took your time,' he said as he held out his hand for the bedroom key.

'Here you are,' Hazel panted as she gave him the key. 'Susan left me a letter I wanted to read. Anyway, I wanted to give you plenty of time to get up here.'

'You do appreciate that we have limited time to get this job done?'

Hazel took a deep breath. 'Listen. I have no idea about your . . . second job . . . nor do I *want* to know about it, Mr. Hunter.'

The gentleman, however, was not listening. He unlocked the door with

121

the key. After a quick peep inside, he allowed her to go in the room first.

Hazel spotted her bag on her bed, just as she'd left it. But the wardrobe door was shut and she was sure she'd left it open. Perhaps Susan had closed it before she'd left? 'You have to get inside the wardrobe,' she explained as she proceeded towards it to open it — but it was locked.

Seeing her struggling to open the wardrobe, Jon gently pushed her to one side and tried to open it himself. 'It's not normal for a hotel wardrobe to be locked with no key available,' he muttered. Taking what looked like a Swiss Army knife from his pocket, he opened up a blade and proceeded to pick the lock.

Fascinated, Hazel watched him. 'I trust you have permission to mutilate the furniture?'

'When needs must,' he replied.

Having opened the wardroom, he produced a very small torch and shone it into the dark inside. 'Can't see any guns,' he muttered.

Hazel pushed him out of the way and climbed inside. 'Let me have your light.' She almost snatched it from his hand; shining it to find the hidden door, she felt for the means to open it.

It might have helped if Jon hadn't squeezed into the wardrobe with her. Hazel wasn't a big woman, but Jon was a fair-sized man, and all muscle — or it seemed like that to squashed Hazel. It might have been embarrassing being so close to him, but both he and Hazel were too busy feeling around the door for the means to open it.

Hazel's fingers found a small swivel catch eventually and the door opened into blackness.

Jon took the torch from Hazel and swung it ahead of him into the attic room. A little light was coming from the skylight above and, as they moved inside the room and their eyes became accustomed to the darkness, they could see the boxes that Hazel had seen there before.

Jon moved in front of her and, crouching down, felt to open one box.

'Blimey!' he exclaimed as the opened box revealed neatly-stacked rifles.

'Told you so!' Hazel was enjoying his discovery — both proving she'd told him the truth, and knowing the guns were of interest to him. He obviously knew about firearms, as he picked one up and examined it with a knowledge-able skill which showed he was familiar with them.

Jon spent a few minutes rummaging about the contents of the boxes — none of which were locked.

'I think,' he said, 'these guns have been here since the war. They are a motley collection of hunting guns — and some German ones, too.'

'Why are they up here?'

'Well, I'm pretty sure they would have been used by the Resistance — the people who were helping the Allies, trying to get rid of the German invaders. Some hid their weapons here, and came to collect them as and when they needed them. For some reason, they've been left.'

Hazel nodded. It seemed like a reasonable explanation.

Jon was testing several of the weapons, and looked around for some ammunition. 'They appear to work — but they may need some attention — God knows how many years they've been here!'

'And who'd want to use them now? Did I tell you that I was half-asleep that night when I was aware that someone crossed the bedroom? I thought I might have been dreaming.'

Jon was sorting out a small collection of rifles and pistols — and boxes with bullets inside them, which he slipped into his pockets.

'Obviously, whoever knew these weapons were here didn't hand them in after the war was over. So I'm afraid it might be criminals who use them now — at least, criminals would like to get their hands on them.'

'Any use to you, for your operation?'

'Indeed. They will look impressive

even if they don't work!'

'Listen!' Hazel said. 'I think I can hear someone calling!'

Jon froze, and put a finger to his mouth to indicate she too must remain quiet.

6

'Whoever is in the bedroom is thrashing about,' Jon commented after they had both listened to the noises of someone looking around and calling. 'You stay here. I'll go and see who it is.'

Hazel didn't like being left in the gloomy attic, but she felt she shouldn't be cowardly and object to being alone for a short time while Jon went to investigate.

Thankfully, it wasn't long before she heard Jon's footsteps returning quickly, and he had someone else with him — Steve.

'Now, listen, Hazel.' Jon caught hold of her and almost whispered in her face, 'We've got to get out of here — sharpish.'

'Why?'

Steve replied, 'I overheard the caretaker phoning the police, reporting the fact that I was going upstairs to your bedroom. She was worried about Hazel being alone up here — the police should be here at any moment.'

Hazel shuddered. 'I thought you were the police!' Surely Jon and Steve weren't criminals?

'The problem we have is that we can't afford the time to explain to the police what we're up to — we've only a short time to meet at the place where the thieves have taken the paintings they've stolen. Unless we get out of here and confront those criminals now, they will get away with those works of art.'

Hazel's eyebrows shot up as she stared at Jon. Could she believe such a cock-and-bull story? Perhaps Jon and Steve were the thieves? Perhaps the police were after *them*? Was she was caught in the middle of this . . . *heist*?

A freezing feeling immobilized Hazel. Coldness gripped her at the thought that she'd fallen into a trap. Jon Hunter had led her into a horrible situation — and she had trusted him!

As she stood feeling aghast, Jon and Steve had been busy arming themselves from the boxes, slinging rifles over their shoulders and stuffing ammunition into their pockets.

'I'll force the skylight window open,' rasped Jon. 'You go and lock the bedroom door. Jam the wardrobe up against it. Then check the back doorway of the wardrobe is shut. That will delay them for some time, I hope — as I don't suppose they will know about this attic chamber entrance — although the Paris police will be familiar with these old buildings, and will soon find out about it.'

After Steve had slipped away, Jon began to move some of the heavy boxes under the skylight window. Taking a couple and putting them on top of each other, he stepped up and, using his hands, thrust them against the skylight.

After much banging and swearing, the window shattered — slivers of glass showered the floor. 'Ah, well!' Jon shouted down to her, after he'd swung himself up through the opening, with the agility of a trained soldier — which, of course, he was. 'That's one way of getting through a window — though you'll have to be very careful not to cut yourself getting through, Hazel.'

She gaped at him. 'Wh-what are you going to do with me?' she stuttered.

'Get up on the boxes as you saw me do, and lift your arms so that I can grab your hands and haul you up.'

Hazel looked around for somewhere to hide. She wasn't part of this operation. The police had nothing on her. She couldn't even speak French, so it was no good them questioning her about what was going on — she didn't know more than that there were a few valuable paintings involved.

'Come on, Hazel, chop-chop — we need to get away.'

Hazel's throat felt dry, and her voice sounded croaky. 'You go . . . '

'Miss Crick!' His deep voice echoed in the attic. 'Get your arse over here, *at once!*'

You could tell he was used to ordering army recruits about. But she was no junior soldier.

'I'm staying *here*,' she shouted back.

He changed his tone. 'Please, Hazel, this is no time to be obstinate — we must get away, or the police will delay us, and we won't be in time to stop the thieves.'

In the silence that followed, she could hear him breathing heavily, and thought he could probably hear her own frantic inhalations.

Again, he called down, 'You must trust me.'

Could she — did she — trust Jon Hunter? A man she'd only known for a short time? And although last night she could have sworn she did have a special relationship with him — and she might have married him if he'd asked her — now the circumstances were very different.

This evening, he was asking her to break the law. Run from the police. And, even worse, to get up onto the roof of a very high building!

'I don't like heights — I suffer from vertigo.' Tears of fear wet her cheeks.

'I'll look after you. Make sure you are safe. Come on — '

'You go — and leave me.'

She could just make out his face looking down on her from above. He spoke more confidentially, 'I understand you don't like heights, but you are going to be with an expert climber. I'll hold onto you and make sure you are safe. It won't take long before you are down on the ground. The chimney sweeps have walkways and ladders on the rooftops that we can use. Come on — if the police get hold of you, they'll put you in prison, and it may take the British Embassy days to get you out.'

That possibility alarmed Hazel — and she did believe he was right about that. She was a simple Englishwoman, with an ordinary family, bought up in wartime, and who now had a good secretarial job. Perhaps she was a stay-at-home sort of girl. Maybe her flaw was that she was not brave and adventurous — nor wanted to be. She preferred to watch scary films at the cinema or on television, certainly not to experience them in reality.

Her hands were perspiring at the thought of being on the roof — she feared her slippery palms would mean she couldn't hold on to the metal ladders, and would . . . fall —

Steve burst into the chamber. 'Get going — now! The police are already battering at the bedroom door,' he shouted urgently. 'I'll follow you.'

'Steve, she won't come with me. Lift her up so I can get hold of her.'

Steve grabbed Hazel's hand and pulled her under the skylight opening, his shoes crunching on the broken glass. With his large hands firmly around her hips, Steve lifted her so that Jon could grasp her arms and pull her up onto the roof.

Hazel was so taken by surprise that Steve was able to lift her up, and that Jon was able to pull her through the window frame, that she could not think in her fright.

'There, Hazel, now all we have to do is to get down,' she heard Jon's reassuring voice murmur near her ear. 'Follow me along this ledge.'

As he was holding tight onto her hand, Hazel had no choice but to walk behind him.

Somehow his hand — which was cool to the touch — had grasped hers so firmly she couldn't have shaken it off even if she'd wanted to. But she was holding on for dear life!

'We're going across to the next house, and then we'll look for the fire escape. Don't worry about Steve; he's as agile as a monkey and will lead the police off our trail.'

As if Hazel could think about anything but the fact that she was way above street level and had a ladder to climb down — by herself!

Strangely, the longer she was up on the roof, the less scared she felt. Or was she so frightened she couldn't think properly?

Windy rain swept the rain hood off

her head, and gusts were blowing her hair about so she couldn't see where she was going. Birds, who'd built their nests up on the roofs, squawked suddenly as they flew off with noisy flapping wings. Hazel felt she was in danger of losing her balance. And when they came out of the shelter of some chimneypots, the wind seemed to want her to fly into the starry night air.

Jon walked on determinedly, half-dragging her along behind him.

'Now, this is the tricky bit,' he announced, stopping.

She wished he hadn't said that, as she was taken by a fit of shivering.

Ignoring her mutterings of fright, he proceeded to explain how they were going to cross onto the adjacent building. 'This is the way the chimney sweeps clambered across — and, I daresay, many a Resistance fighter during the war.'

He sounded so confident. She shuddered. What was easy for him didn't make it any easier for her.

'Now, I want you to stay here and wait for a moment or two — '

Where else could she go? Hazel thought bitterly. She wished she was safely at home in bed, not walking on the rooftops of Paris!

Whatever manoeuvre he made, he did it quickly, with professional skill, and was ahead of her a few seconds later, saying, 'Hold on to this rifle, I've got the other end of it. Now, take small sideward steps toward me — and don't look down!'

What choice did she have? Hazel's nerves were raw. But she had trusted him so far, and no harm had come to her, so hadn't she better continue? She certainly couldn't go back, and didn't want to spend the rest of the night in this draughty, dangerous place.

'That's my girl,' she heard him say, and she did as she was told and edged forward and into his arms. That was a lovely feeling — to have his arms around her, his hand rubbing her back to comfort her.

'Now we only have to climb down the fire escape. I'll go first, and you follow me, and you'll find there's a little landing at each floor down, so you can have a rest as we go.'

It was easier than Hazel had imagined it would be. The fire escape had been designed for people to exit a burning building, so the handrail was easy to grasp, and the steps — though steep — were not difficult to descend. Even so, her legs felt wobbly when they reached the pavement at last.

They were not in the front of the building, but in a dimly-lit narrow alleyway.

'Come on, we've got to make a run for it.' Jon gave her no time to recover. 'Here, push this rifle under your mac so no one will see it.'

She found the gun was a heavy object, and awkward to have to carry. Realizing that Jon had been carrying two rifles, she made no protest, and tried her best to conceal it under her coat.

He clasped her to him, and they walked out of the alley. Soon they were amongst people walking along the street. With everyone keeping their heads down in the blustery weather, the guns they were carrying didn't attract attention from anyone.

A church clock rang out the time, and Jon said, 'I think we might still make it.'

Hazel, who was in danger of tripping over her rifle as she was hustled along, felt a slight sense of achievement — she obviously hadn't prevented Jon from continuing with his operation. Although unclear as to what it was all about, she had the impression it meant a lot to him to finish it.

Having been escorted along several streets, she was suddenly stopped and pushed into a doorway.

'I've spotted a suspect, and I don't want him to see me,' Jon said in a hushed voice.

Hazel was almost breathless after the forced march. Quietly, she whispered back, 'I'll stay here while you carry on and follow him.'

'I need you with your rifle.'

'I can't use a gun!'

'They won't know that. Just do as I say.'

'They will see I'm young and small in size — young ladies are taught to dance and do needlework, not to use firearms.'

'Of course many women can — especially some French women during the war. They fought with the Resistance. Anyway, these robbers won't care who is at the end of a rifle if it's pointing at them.'

Hazel digested what he'd told her. But her hands were shaking just holding the rifle — she shuddered. In a small, frightened voice, she said, 'I'm sorry, Jon, I don't think I can shoot anyone.'

He gave a huge sigh. 'I'm not asking you to *use* the gun. Point it at 'em — that's all you'll need to do.'

'But who and where are these crooks?'

'They are a group of men — '

'Jon — how many of them are there? There are only two of us.'

'Steve will be joining us, and a group of security men too — all trained fighters. The thieves are a few men who are employed — or have accomplices who are — unwrapping and hanging valuable pictures in the museum galleries; pictures that have been stored over the war years. They're not likely to be armed. Or, if they are, we should be able to overpower them.'

Satisfied that they were not going to be outnumbered, or that she would have to fire the rifle, Hazel calmed down a bit. She longed to say that she felt exhausted — she'd had long periods of walking she wasn't used to that day. She really only wanted to sit down and have a cup of tea. Chasing criminals was not her forte.

But what if Jon was telling the truth, and some thieves were planning to steal some art masterpieces? And he was genuinely trying to stop them? Surely she should be willing to help him, tired though she was. She loved painting, and knew how skilled the Old Masters were. Their work should be for everyone to be able to see and enjoy — not just a few art collectors who paid people to steal some for them.

In the darkened doorway she was able to see his face — a face she loved. Commanding, yes, but compassionate too — she hadn't been let down by him, had she? He'd made sure she'd been well taken care of — and, after all, it wasn't his fault she'd been put in his car and had to be taken to France, was it?

Now he was asking her to help him out with the important job he had to do. He wasn't going to steal the paintings — no, his task was to rescue them.

Making up her mind quickly, she said, 'All right. I believe you are in the middle of an important investigation to prevent some artwork being stolen. And I'm prepared to help you if I can.'

He bent down and kissed her cold lips. 'Thank you, Hazel. As I said earlier, we may be too late — but we can give it a try, eh?'

She nodded, wondering what she'd let herself in for.

He glanced at the street. 'Steve should be here by now. I think we'd better get on with it — '

'What do you want me to do?'

'Come with me. Do exactly as I say.'

That sounded simple enough. However, Hazel didn't expect his next move, which was to tug off the lid of a nearby manhole and say, 'We're going down here.'

From the rooftops to the sewers of Paris!

Hazel stared down the hole Jon had revealed. It was as uninviting as being asked to walk into a prison. But she told herself that she'd volunteered to assist him, and she couldn't back out of it now.

'There's a ladder at the side — see it? Climb down — you'll see it's quite well-lit down there — and wait for me at the bottom.'

Once again, Hazel felt she was taking her life in her hands. But she obediently sat on the edge of the manhole, and edged herself in to feel the handgrip and the ladder steps.

'Here goes.' She told herself it wasn't the time to complain about the dirt or the stink she feared she would encounter.

Down and down she climbed, much further than she thought she'd have to go. Jon, she was aware, was following her, and it made the descent less frightening.

Reaching the hard floor at the bottom of the shaft, she stepped aside so that Jon could climb down and stand beside her.

Rushing water could be heard, and the good lighting enabled her to see the network of underground tunnels.

'Come this way.' Jon seemed to know his way around, and ushered her along until they came to a maintenance room. He used a key to open the door and they walked inside a long passage with dials on the walls, which looked to Hazel like a control area.

'There they are!' Jon's voice sounded triumphant as he walked up to a small box which had been placed at eye-level on top of a tank.

His hand stretched out to grasp the box. Using his Swiss Army knife, he prised it open.

'Six miniatures,' he crowed with delight. Picking one small package out of the box, he proceeded to unwrap it to confirm that a small painting was really there. 'Now, we'll put these in my pockets for safekeeping — here are two for you to keep safe, so put them in your handbag. I trust Steve will be along any minute with the cigarette packets that will replace them in the box so that the thieves will not suspect they are not there.'

Hazel would have loved to see the valuable little paintings, which she presumed were portraits, as miniatures usually were. But there was no time, and Jon was on edge waiting for Steve to join them and set up the trick to fool the thieves.

The waiting seemed interminable to Hazel. Looking at Jon pacing the floor and continually at his watch made her feel edgy. Clearly this was a very important job to him. His body showed he was tense. His whole attention was absorbed by what was about to happen.

Certainly, she seemed to be invisible to him. Although she would have liked to be even nearer him — taken in his arms for reassurance — she knew his mind was elsewhere.

It struck Hazel that this was not just a job of catching thieves; it seemed to her that it was somehow personal to him. These small paintings — miniatures — meant more to him than just their monetary value.

'God, I wish they would hurry!' he muttered.

They? Hazel wondered how many they might have to confront, and shivered.

Hearing footsteps approaching, Jon

called to her, 'Get your rifle ready to use.'

She was shaken to see he had a pistol in his hand as he moved behind the open door and beckoned her to join him.

With a thumping heart, Hazel rushed to stand behind him.

7

Mr. Percival Payne, the principal of Highminster Community College in England, had just arrived home, placed his backside down in his cushioned armchair, and settled his slippered feet on his footstool. Picking up the Sunday newspaper, he began to look at the headlines — when the phone rang in the hall.

The shuffle of feet told him that his wife had gone to answer it. He expected it was her sister, Sylvia, who carried on endless conversations on the phone almost daily.

'Percy,' his wife called, 'it's for you.'

Reluctantly, he rose; and asked as he went out into the hall, 'Who is it?'

'Mr. Crick,' she answered handing him the receiver. 'Your secretary's father.'

'Hello, Mr. Crick, what can I do for you?'

'Sorry to bother you this evening,

Mr. Payne, but I wondered if you knew where Hazel, my daughter, is?'

Mr. Payne hadn't the foggiest, and said so.

Hazel's father then gave a garbled story about Hazel being in Paris this weekend. And she was expected home hours ago and hadn't turned up. He ended by saying, 'Time is getting on, and I thought I'd better warn you that she may not be in for work tomorrow.'

'Oh dear! There's a lot of typing I wanted her to do — I suppose I'll have to get a temp in. Anyway, thank you for letting me know.'

Putting down the phone with a puzzled expression on his face, Mr. Payne muttered, 'I hope she's all right; she's a first-class secretary, and I'd hate to lose her.'

A little later, when his wife bought him in a cup of tea, he asked her, 'What do you think my secretary is doing in Paris this weekend?'

'You mean that pretty young thing, Hazel Crick?'

148

'Miss Crick is a respectable girl.'

His wife smiled. 'Well, I can think of many things I'd like to do if I was in Paris this weekend — even if I was *respectable*, as you put it — and hurrying back to Highminster isn't one of them!'

Mr. Payne scowled. 'One's job should come first. If Hazel Crick can't be reliable, then I'll have to replace her,' he muttered.

★   ★   ★

If Mr. Payne had but known it, Hazel would have loved to be back home safely in Highminster. The only comfort she had in her present dangerous position in the smelly sewers of Paris was that she was with Jon — and for some reason, he gave her confidence.

Moments later, as the footsteps they heard came nearer, Steve called, 'Are you there, sir?'

Jon retorted, 'Hush, for goodness' sake, man.' His arm shot out as he yanked Steve into the room and asked anxiously, 'Have you got the cigarette packets?'

'Yes, sir. Here they are — and you owe me for the cost of them.'

Jon took them and said, 'Take the cigarettes out of the packets quickly — now, what can we put in the packets so that they are not empty and weigh a little heavier?'

'Sand?' suggested Hazel.

The men looked at her astonishment.

'Yes,' she said. 'There are some fire buckets full of sand about — I've noticed them. You'll only need a couple of handfuls — that should be enough, I'd think.'

'Brilliant idea!' Steve praised her, which made her feel useful. For the next five minutes, they were busy doing as Hazel suggested. The filled cigarette packets replaced the miniatures that had been taken from the box, and the box itself was returned to where they had found it.

'Now I suggest we make ourselves

scarce. Position ourselves a little way from here, and hope Security arrives when the thieves pick up the box, so we don't have to arrest them.'

'How many are in this plot?' asked Steve as they left the room and walked down the corridor to decide where they were going to conceal themselves.

Jon said, 'I don't know exactly — but only one or two will come to collect the box, I expect. Then it will be passed on to other criminals — a network that has been successfully spiriting away works of art and selling the stuff abroad. It would be great if we were able to arrest several of them tonight.'

It was a cold and miserable wait that night in the dark, evil-smelling sewer. Crouched in a shadow behind a pillar, Hazel soon felt desperately tired and cold, despite her coat. Her fingers didn't want to keep holding onto her rifle. Her eyes wanted to close and her feet felt like blocks of ice.

Jon and Steve had stationed them-selves a little way from her, so she could get no reassurance from either of them.

She only hoped the miniature paintings she had in her handbag were worth all the suffering she was enduring. But she was aware that she'd changed from being a scared mouse to a rat with teeth. She was going to stick it out for Jon's sake — even if it killed her!

After what seemed like hours, they heard men's voices and feet walking towards them. Two ordinary-looking working men in grimy overalls — probably maintenance staff — walked by them and went towards the room they were keeping an eye on.

When they emerged, one was carrying the box of cigarettes packets! They were obviously the thieves disguised as workmen, and knew exactly where the box had been placed for collection. Thank goodness they hadn't checked the contents! They didn't given the impression that they were in any hurry, and anyone meeting them might have thought that they were carrying a lunchbox — certainly nothing of value.

Suddenly, bedlam broke loose. Shouts and cries echoed in the underground passage as Jon and Steve emerged from their hiding places and challenged the thieves — who, on seeing only two men confronting them, decided to fight their way out. Fists flew at each other, and bloodied faces were soon evident.

In the confusion, Hazel stepped out and pointed her gun at the fighting men. Although initially afraid to use it in case she shot Jon or Steve, she then remembered she didn't know how to fire it anyway — or even if it had any bullets in it.

One of the thieves managed to floor Steve and made to grab the box; but Hazel saw her opportunity to help, stood over it, and pointed her rifle at him.

When he hesitated, Jon came from behind him and dragged him with a rugby tackle to the ground. Amid French curses, and the sounds of thumps and cries, they fought to get the better of each other.

Hazel began to sway; confusion

prevented her from knowing exactly what was happening, although she was aware of guns being fired and other men coming to join the fight.

All this violence, blood and anger over six little paintings — she wondered if they could possibly be worth it.

★　★　★

Hazel thought she must have fainted.

All was quiet around her — and she was comfortable, lying down with a warm blanket over her. The chatter around her was in French, so she couldn't understand what was being said.

Who had won the fight? Who was carrying her on a stretcher? Where were they taking her?

But all she really wanted to know was, *Is Jon safe?* And Steve too, of course?

She had only a vague awareness of having being transported, and it frightened her to feel so weak and helpless.

She could make out some uniformed men, and at one stage had had the impression that she was in a lift.

The cold evening air told her she was up out of the sewers ... Soon, she became aware of being outside in the street with the noise of traffic, flashing lights, and many people about.

'*Mademoiselle.*' An older uniformed man with a French accent had crouched down to speak to her. ''Ave you a pain?'

Hazel shook her head, not able to describe the weakness and discomfort her body was experiencing.

'Can you sit up if I 'elp you?'

Only by trying, thought Hazel, and did so by raising herself on her elbows.

'*Bon!*' the man said with an encouraging smile as she managed to sit up. 'Now, can you stand, perhaps?'

Another policeman was there, anxious to assist her, and Hazel decided they were not acting as if they were about to put handcuffs on her and arrest her.

'*Voila!*' Hazel received more praise as

she placed her feet on the floor and held on to the large hands that were offered to help her stand.

She felt wobbly, and was glad she was being supported by the two French officers. They sat her on a chair that someone provided, and she looked around anxiously for a sighting of Jon or Steve. But they were nowhere to be seen amongst the throng of policemen and curious people on the street who stopped and stared, commented, and then moved on.

Whatever had happened while she was unconscious? The sting she'd taken part in seemed to be at an end.

Who had won? What had happened to the thieves and the works of art?

And, more importantly, what had happened to Jon? Her eyes kept searching for him while she tried to quell horrid ideas that floated into her mind about his fate.

There he was! She spied him talking to some officers, and when they pointed to Hazel he came striding over and crouched down to take her hands and speak to her. 'How are you, Hazel — were you hurt in the scuffle?'

Hazel gulped. Scuffle? To her, it had seemed as though they were fighting for their lives — although she couldn't remember any shots being fired.

'I'm OK. But I can see you're injured. Your face is bleeding — '

'Yep. I do need patching up.'

She stroked his bloodied face gently with her fingers, knowing he must be suffering.

'Sorry I had to leave you, Hazel,' he said. 'I needed to talk to the police — '

'Are they going to arrest us?'

He smiled lifted one of her hands, putting it to his lips gallantly. 'No. They came to help us. Don't you remember Steve telling us that the caretaker at your hotel called the police? She was concerned about you with a man in your room. And we had to get away from the police as they would have delayed us, and we would have been unable to get on with the operation to save the paintings.'

'Oh!' It all sounded a bit muddled to Hazel. 'Are the paintings safe?'

'Well, I have four of them in my pocket — which I hope are still intact. Ouch!' He attempted to check, but the obvious pain he felt in his arm prevented him from doing so. Hazel looked sympathetically at his swollen, battered face and hands. He would have a black eye in the morning, and kept dabbing a split lip with his handkerchief. She felt so sorry to see him hurt.

'I have two of the paintings in my handbag — wherever that is.' Hazel's eyes looked round for it.

He assured her, 'All your things are with the police — quite safe.'

She presumed they were — she trusted him, didn't she? She put her hand out to gently stroke his untidy hair — of course she trusted him.

His lips tenderly touched hers. 'Now, I must go to hospital to be patched up, with Steve.'

'Is Steve badly hurt?'

'He'll live.'

'What shall I do?'

'Do you want to go to hospital, Hazel?'

She shook her head. 'As far as I know, I'm still in one piece. Just tired, sore, and bewildered. I don't want to go back to my hotel.'

'I thought so. A plain-clothes police-woman — who knows a little English — has offered to take you to my hotel, where you can have a bath and a good night's sleep in a comfortable bed.'

That sounded wonderful, and her anxiety slipped from her. It was typical of him to make sure she was well taken care of. 'Thanks,' she said.

'It is I who should thank you, Hazel. Without your bravery, the operation would have not been successful.' He tried to give her a smile, but she could appreciate it wasn't possible with his injured face.

He rose to his feet stiffly and walked towards a policewoman who was approaching them. He talked to the officer for a short time, turned to Hazel and gave her a wave, and then walked towards the ambulance which had just drawn up.

Her heart lurched as Jon left her. She wanted to yell out, *Don't leave me — ever!*

After some difficulty in understanding each other, and a chuckle or two, the French policewoman escorted Hazel to a waiting car, and the two of them sped off to Jon's hotel.

It was a grand hotel they entered. Hazel was still suffering from shock, and trembled as she was escorted into the lobby. Would they throw her out in her untidy state, thinking she was drunk? They might wonder why the policewoman had brought her to this classy hotel, when she was sure there were many hotels in Paris that, whilst they might not have been as decrepit as the one she Susan and were in, were less expensive.

To her amazement, she spied a porter carrying her handbag and all the luggage she'd left at the other hotel. It was a relief to know she had not lost them.

They were taken up in a lift to a wide corridor which smelled of furniture polish. A uniformed maid was waiting at the door of a room that was opened.

Going inside, Hazel knew it was Jon's room, as a few of his personal possessions could be seen.

The policewoman said, in halting English, 'First you take a bath, eh? Then you will have something to eat before you go to bed?'

It sounded like luxury to Hazel, and she readily agreed.

As a result of her rather spartan upbringing, the kind of simple bathroom she was used to did had not prepared her for this mirrored, shining room, with its huge tub and a separate shower, plus the adjoining toilet and bidet. She just stood for a moment to admire it as the policewoman ran the taps that began to spurt hot water.

She was offered a choice of bath oils

and shrugged, not knowing which one to choose. So the policewoman removed the top of one or two, and gave them to Hazel to sniff.

'It doesn't matter which one,' Hazel exclaimed, 'any perfume would be better than the smell of the sewers!' The policewoman dolloped some liquid from an ornate bottle into the bath-water, saying 'It's a pretty colour. You'll 'ave a good smell of flowers.'

Lying in the pleasantly hot bath with bubbly foam up to her neck, it became difficult to stay awake. And if the policewoman hadn't stood by the tub with a fluffy bath towel, Hazel may well have stayed in the tub all night.

A waiter wheeled in a trolley of food Hazel didn't recognize — unless the chef had decorated it so that she didn't. But a bowl of hot *potage* with a French roll tasted delicious; refusing wine, she settled for white coffee, urging the policewoman to join her in the repast.

The soft bed she was put in sent her to sleep immediately.

★　★　★

Hazel's parents waited anxiously for news of their daughter, who hadn't turned up on Sunday evening as they'd been told by Mr. Hunter she would.

Molly, Hazel's mother, said to her husband over breakfast, 'It's not like Hazel to be unreliable — in fact, she is so reliable, it makes me more worried not knowing where and how she is.'

Her father, William, tried not to show his concern. 'She's young and healthy, Molly; I doubt if any harm's come to her.'

'I'd just like to know.'

'Maybe we'll hear soon.'

As the morning wore on, though, all they received was a phone call from the college principal, who sounded peeved. He informed them that, as Hazel hadn't turned up for work, he'd had to hire temporary office help — and from the sound of his voice, the lady who had come to replace Hazel hadn't a clue, and he really missed his usual secretary's efficiency.

This compliment was appreciated by her parents — until he went on to say, 'I'll have to hire another girl, there is work piling up that needs to be done.'

'I'm sure Hazel will be with you tomorrow, Mr. Payne,' William tried to reassure the principal. 'Staff do take occasional days off with flu — '

'If she's unwell, she should have let me know, Mr. Crick.'

What could William reply to that? He knew Mr. Payne was right. 'I'll let you know as soon as we hear something,' was all he could say.

'Should we ring the French Embassy?' Molly suggested, with a concerned look on her face.

'Let's wait a bit longer, dear. You know our Hazel won't be doing anything daft — like consorting with criminals!'

★ ★ ★

Monday morning in Paris was gloriously warm. The rainclouds had gone, the bright sunshine lit the elegant city as if no crime could ever mar its beauty, and the birds sang happily, making everyone feel life was a privilege.

Hazel woke from a sound sleep and didn't feel she wanted to rise.

She probably wouldn't have if she hadn't heard a familiar male voice from the sitting room. 'Wake up, sleepyhead.'

Hazel sat up, bombarded by recollections of her adventure yesterday — and the sudden realization that she should be at work. Goodness — whatever was the time?

Someone had drawn back the long window drapes, and that someone was standing in the bedroom doorway with a cup of coffee in his hand.

'Jon!' she cried, delighted to see him. His face was partly covered with bandages and one of his arms was in a sling.

He walked into the bedroom and placed the cup of coffee in her hands, saying, 'Drink this and get up — it's time for lunch.'

With that, he turned and walked out

of the bedroom, shutting the door behind him.

Hazel would have liked him to stay — there were so many questions she wanted to ask him. But she knew she had to get up.

Someone had valeted her clothes, and fresh underwear was laid out for her, so she didn't take long to dash into the bathroom for a quick wash — her toothbrush and toothpaste were there ready for her to use. It wasn't until she'd combed her hair and looked in the mirror to see that she was presentable that she thought about her parents — they would be worried about her.

Walking quickly into the sitting room, where Jon was reading a newspaper, she said, 'My dad and mum will be worried about me. Can I phone them immediately?'

Jon put down the paper and said, 'Well, I did, and they were. But don't worry, they know you are safe and well.'

'What about my boss, Mr. Payne?'

'Your parents told me they had contacted him.'

Hazel was relieved to hear that.

'And Steve — is he OK?'

'He tells me he is. He's been spending the day at the Louvre doing my job.'

'He wasn't hurt last night in the fight?'

'Steve is a better fighter than I am. He got away with minor injuries. Now, as it is a glorious autumn day — what's left of it — and you missed your sightseeing with Susan yesterday, and it is too late for me to deliver the paintings . . . let me show you around Paris.'

Being with him and being shown Paris was a treat Hazel could not refuse, although she asked, 'Are you able to? I mean, you've been hurt — '

'A few cuts and scratches. A restful day of sightseeing will be just what the doctor ordered, I assure you.'

Examining him, Hazel realized he was more injured than he wanted to admit. His eye was black and blue, and his mouth swollen. And his arm — had it been broken?

'When will we return to Highminster? Mr. Payne won't appreciate me being away for long — there's a great deal of work to be done — '

'I understand he's hired a temp.'

'That won't suit Mr. Payne — he's a stickler!'

Jon said, 'He will appreciate you all the more when you return to work.'

'I suppose so . . . '

'Hazel, you are entitled to some days off work — holidays are important for staff to refresh themselves.'

'Not taking days off whenever you feel like it, and letting your employer down!'

'But you haven't! What has happened to you was as unforeseen as a bout of flu attacking you — and perhaps worse, eh?'

Hazel wasn't sure about that. Flu — or any painful condition — could be very unpleasant to suffer. And she wouldn't deny that she had suffered in the last few days. But, also, something wonderful had happened to her: she'd fallen in love.

Right now, she was able to be with the man she loved, and he was offering to take her out to see the famous sights of Paris. How fortunate she was! Let the future take care of itself — she would take advantage of this time and enjoy it.

Her next concern was his condition: he was using his injured arm gingerly. 'I see you have one arm out of action — is it painful for you to get around? Shouldn't you be resting it?'

He grimaced. 'Can't say it doesn't give me a twinge every now and again: it certainly does. But as far as I'm concerned, I'd rather be out and about with you than languishing on a sofa.'

'All right,' she said, delighted he did not want to cancel the outing. 'But promise me you'll let me know if your arm becomes too painful and you need to rest it.'

He obviously wanted to ignore his sore arm, and as they were going to travel on public transport, he assured her he could manage — simply being with her would give him pleasure.

'Thanks,' Hazel said sincerely, as she too knew she would appreciate his company.

As she had anticipated, Hazel spent a day to remember with Jon. She was conscious of him being sore and tired, although he tried to hide it. What amazed her was that he was so knowledgeable about France and Paris. They didn't need a guide — he was well-informed about everything they saw.

They saw so much: the Eiffel Tower, Arc de Triomphe, Tomb of Napoleon, Notre-Dame, and much more. Hazel enjoyed not only experiencing being at these famous places, but hearing Jon's voice telling her about them and his jokey remarks.

Something was bothering him, though — she felt sure he was on the alert. He kept his eyes looking around as if he was expecting some . . . trouble?

In the end, she asked him, 'Will the art criminals kick back at you?'

He gave her a wry, lopsided smile. 'Those that weren't caught by the police yesterday will no doubt take a pot shot at me if they get the chance.'

'So that is why you live in England?'

'Partly. Although the Brits have their fair share of criminals too.'

'You keep looking over your shoulder — are you in danger right now?'

He chuckled. 'I still have the miniatures they want.'

'Did you leave them in the hotel?'

He patted his jacket pocket. 'I have them with me — and, just to reassure you, I also have a bodyguard. Look, he's over there, pretending to be searching for something in his tourist guidebook.'

Hazel looked to where Jon was pointing. Sure enough, the man waved back at her.

'Is he armed?'

'Yes, and Sam Butler is a crack shot too.'

Hazel was thoughtful, then said, 'I'm surprised the French government pay for people like you to protect their artwork.'

'Ah, but the French love and value art. And works of art are worth millions of francs.'

Hazel smiled at him, because she too valued art.

She asked him, 'Do you have a bodyguard when you're in England?'

He shook his head. 'Only in Paris at the moment, because there are still a few disgruntled burglars around who may want to eliminate me.'

She shuddered as he went on to explain, 'The security department are being cautious; they think I am vulnerable, unable to fully defend myself at present. But I assure you I'm fine.'

However, she began to detect a tiredness creeping over him. Like a good nurse, she knew when he'd had enough and needed to rest, and said so.

'Let's eat at the hotel this evening,

shall we?' he suggested. 'Then we can go straight to bed — I think we both need a good night's rest.'

She agreed readily, thinking of his need to recuperate.

So Jon hired room service when they returned to the hotel. They ate a splendid meal, and went out onto the hotel balcony to drink their after-dinner wine and look out over the city of Paris in the evening light.

Close together, Hazel liked to feel his hand around her and his lips touch her neck. 'Hazel, I think you know I'm most grateful to you for having stood by me last night — '

'I didn't have much choice, I seem to remember.'

'Well, no, I suppose the way things worked out you didn't. But you could have made the whole operation impossible for me. I could see you were scared — battling against fatigue, cold and miserable at the end before you fainted.'

'I could tell it was important to you,

Jon. And I was determined to stick by you. But you got the worst of it.'

'Yes, well, I'm a trained soldier.'

'I'm just glad it all worked out — '

'It hasn't finished yet.'

Hazel turned her head to look questioningly into his jewel-like eyes.

He took the opportunity to place his lips gently on hers, unable to kiss her properly with his injured mouth. But for Hazel, the feel of him was electric — comforting to be in his strong arms — sensual to be joined to him even for a few seconds.

She knew he couldn't give her a passionate caress with his sore lips, but she loved the feel of the gentle kiss. It was beyond any kiss she'd ever experienced because she felt he was making love to her — he meant her to know it. For a few seconds she belonged to him — but did he belong to her?

Before she could question him about what else he had to do, and what arrangements he'd made for tomorrow, he released her. Taking her by the hand, he took her indoors and indicated that she was to retire to his bedroom.

Momentarily thinking he wanted her to spend the night with him, she wondered what she would say; but he informed her, 'I have another bedroom lined up along the corridor. Goodnight, my dear.'

'Thanks for the lovely day sightseeing in this beautiful city.'

'Glad you enjoyed yourself, Hazel; so did I.'

He left her to enjoy her sweet dreams of him.

8

Once again, Hazel slept well in the luxury hotel bed and awoke refreshed. However, the day's problems soon overtook her feeling of wellbeing. Realizing her present situation of being pampered was about to end, she wondered when — and how — she was going to get home.

As she showered and dressed, she wondered too how Jon was today. Although he'd given her a memorable tour of Paris yesterday, and seemed happy that his plan to thwart the art thieves had been successful, she was sure he was still suffering from his wounded body after his fight with them. Was he going to stay in Paris for a while, and leave her to go back to England on her own?

Hazel now felt able to do this. Her experiences in France had matured her, made her less scared of coping with the unknown — it was a sense of achievement that pleased her. Being born in a provincial English town, with her youth restricted as to where she could go because of the war, it was understandable that she had a lot to learn.

Looking at the clock, she was horrified to see the time — almost midday. Once again, there was no hope of her getting to work. Mr. Payne would be mad with her. He liked things done like clockwork — and so did she — but even a good temporary secretary wouldn't know her filing system, or even where the paperclips were kept.

It was imperative she got back to work as soon as possible.

Having washed and dressed, she wondered if there was a ferry to England she could catch. Then she could get a train or bus to Highminster. At least she would be able to be back at her desk by tomorrow morning. She must discuss her departure from France with Jon, in case he had to book some tickets.

She wondered which room Jon was in. Perhaps she should ring Reception and find out.

She picked up the phone receiver and was about to dial, hoping the receptionist could speak English.

'Good morning, Miss Crick,' the female receptionist answered, in English with a French accent.

Hazel was taken aback, until she reflected that a first-class international hotel such as the one she was in would certainly employ staff that could speak one or two languages — and English in particular, as they would have many American visitors.

'I would like to know which room Mr. Hunter is in, please.'

'We 'aven't a Mr. 'unter staying 'ere, Miss Crick.'

Funny, thought Hazel. She was sure Jon had told her that he would be in a room along her corridor.

'Are you sure?' Hazel asked.

'I'm looking at the guest book, and I cannot see a Mr. 'unter.'

'Well, he was using this room I am in, the night before last — yes, Friday night he was definitely here.'

''Old on, Madame, I'll ask the manager.'

When the receptionist returned to the phone, she told Hazel that the only guest that had occupied the room she was in before her was the Comte de la Fare.

Hazel thanked her and rang off, thinking that perhaps she had misunderstood Jon, and that he had gone to another hotel as there were several nearby.

But she was worried. How would she find him? She needed to borrow some more money to pay for her fare home.

She didn't have to worry long as, when someone tapped on the suite door, there he was.

'Hello,' he said, smiling as best he could with his still-swollen mouth. 'You look a trifle bothered — is there anything wrong?'

'Hello, Jon. I'm fine now after sleeping in your comfortable bed. Although still a little shaken by all that has happened to me in the last few days. Are you feeling better this morning?'

'Not too bad. You look fresh as a daisy. May I come in?'

In her bewilderment she'd forgotten her manners. 'Yes, of course, do come in.' She was about to add, 'It's your hotel suite!' But was it?

'Have you ordered breakfast?' he asked as he strode in and dropped down comfortably in an easy chair — he certainly behaved as though he owned the room.

'No,' she replied.

He picked up the phone and asked the dining room to bring them up some breakfast — and it struck Hazel that he'd assumed his normal air of authority.

She sat on the edge of a chair and asked hesitantly, 'Where did you spend the night?'

He looked at her, slightly surprised. 'Here. Number one hundred and eight.'

She shifted on her chair and murmured, 'Reception told me they hadn't a Mr. Hunter in the hotel; that's why I asked you.'

He gave a snort of a laugh. 'Checking up on me, were you?'

Hazel frowned. 'No. Curious, that's all. Ever since I've known you, you've always kept something up your sleeve — which, of course, is your business. But I don't like being lied to. I wanted to ask you — '

He boomed, 'I've never lied to you!'

'Just kept me in the dark.'

He sighed. 'I had my work to do — you gate-crashed it.'

'I didn't want to get involved — it was circumstances — I wasn't to know you have two lives!'

He didn't seem to have an answer to that accusation — nor did he offer an explanation.

She pressed her lips together, then said crossly, 'I simply want to go home — correction, I *have* to go home. And I wanted you to lend me some more money, I'm afraid, as I can't afford the tickets for it. I was not trying to snoop on you, if that's what you think, I merely wanted to ask you how I can return to England today.'

'Ah. That's difficult.'

Hazel saw red. 'It isn't difficult at all! You brought me here against my will. Now you get me back to England.'

His normal disposition had turned to something like anger. 'I seem to remember it wasn't me that put you in my car. I certainly didn't put you there. It was *you* who became a millstone around my neck, just as I was about to complete an important mission. You who offered to help me after you'd wandered off and got lost in Paris. My God, Hazel, don't blame me for your present situation — which is far from being catastrophic!'

As he paused to take a breath after his outburst, Hazel chipped in, 'Don't blame me for your zeal to rescue the little miniatures — I just happened to get in your way. That's all. These unfortunate things happen.'

'Hazel,' he thundered, 'I get paid by the French Government to protect their works of art. I'm at risk from criminals who would kill me. It is not just my sense of *zeal*, as you put it. If I'm obliged to hide my identity or avoid revealing my operations, then it's because it is necessary.' He took a deep breath. 'I haven't hurt you — or ever wanted to.'

Hazel felt a little scared of him. He was right — up to a point. 'It doesn't give you the right to keep me here.'

'I don't intend to keep you here. We are going down to my mother's house today.'

Now Hazel felt alarmed. 'Oh, are we?' she said icily.

'Yes. I have accepted the invitation — and for you too.'

Hazel got up and walked towards the door — she had in mind to make a run for it, go to the police and say she was being kidnapped. But the door had opened and a waiter was pushing in a trolley with their breakfast on it,

183

blocking her way out.

'Stop being so dramatic, Hazel, and sit down. Then we'll discuss what I have in mind — and if you insist on leaving France today, I dare say I can fix you up on a night ferry . . . but Mama will be disappointed not to meet you.'

That sounded more conciliatory, and as the waiter was offering her a plate with a napkin and a delicious-looking croissant, she relented. Having been provided with a large cup of coffee as well, Hazel waited until the waiter had checked that they were well served before he left the room.

Jon munched his croissant as if she didn't exist. He dunked it in his coffee — a horrid French habit, she thought, as the melted chocolate ran down the side of his cup: he slurped it up appreciatively. She watched him for a while and sighed. Would she ever understand him? Then she felt hungry and decided to have her breakfast, too.

As she ate she began to think it was a shame they were at loggerheads.

What a reasonable man he really was. He hadn't attempted to seduce her. He had paid out God knew how much for her to be comfortable and entertained during her stay in Paris — and he was offering to put her on the ferry this evening. The sum of it was, he hadn't invited her to Paris. He'd had a job to do here, and he'd done it. He'd not been responsible for her being tangled up with the criminals he was after — so she shouldn't be blaming him that she was still in Paris.

Watching him furtively over her coffee cup, she loved the look of him. Admired his mellow male voice and quirky smile — although his face was a little distorted with the battering it had received. Normally, he had the visage of a handsome, mature man. But in the cross mood he was in now, she noticed the darkness under his eyes. Had showing her around Paris been a little too much for him, when he really needed to take things easy to recover? Was his arm bothering him more than he admitted? Had he a headache, or other injuries she couldn't see?

Thanks to him, she'd had two comfortable nights in one of the best hotels in Paris when he could have left her in that attic bedroom alone — oh, indeed she wouldn't have liked that at all!

Deep in her heart, she knew she wasn't being fair to him. She still had a lot to learn about him. She needed more time to really get to know him better, to get answers to some of the questions she had about him. Perhaps it was plain curiosity — nosiness — because she knew very well that an experienced man like him would not be interested in a permanent relationship with a simple girl like herself. However, if he was to be working in Highminster as an Arts and Environmental officer, she would be seeing him occasionally . . .

Did she want to end her stay in Paris on a sour note — blaming him for what had happened?

Impulsively, she said, 'Sorry, Jon. I

know you have done a lot for me, and I am most grateful.'

He seemed to have got over his ill humour too, and smiled at her. 'As I've said before, it is I who want to thank you for making my operation work.'

They looked at each other somewhat sheepishly, feeling ashamed of their tiff, yet knowing there were many things that had to be sorted out between them.

Jon got up and went to one of the long windows and looked out. With his back to her he said, 'You must decide if you want to go back to England this evening. I can arrange it, and make sure the guard on the train keeps an eye on you until you reach the channel ferry. I'll book you a night cabin on board the ferry, and in the early morning you'll be in England. Trains run regularly to London from the port — which is where the majority of passengers go. And from there you'll be able to get a bus or train on to Highminster. I have a temporary passport for you — and, of course, I'll make sure you have enough money with you for the journey. It shouldn't be a problem for an intelligent young lady like you.'

Hazel gulped. It sounded as though he meant what he said. Had he decided to get rid of her?

He swung around to face her. 'But . . . if you decide to come with me to visit my mother, which I hope you will, then you will go to England with me a day later — and we'll fly.'

There, the choice was clear.

Finding it difficult to express what she felt about him and his proposal, she began to ponder what to do. 'I suppose if I *had* had flu, Mr. Payne wouldn't have me in the office for two or three days anyway . . . '

He took over where she left off. 'And you'll be much more refreshed after a short flight, rather than after a long train and ferry crossing . . . '

And I'll be with you, she thought silently, thinking how she would miss the security and warmth of his companionship.

Before her was a once-in-a-lifetime choice — no one could tell her what to do — she had to decide. It was up to her to prolong her stay in France, something she would always treasure if she did. She had already acquired some memories of Paris she would always value.

'I will come with you, Jon,' she said quietly and firmly.

He came up to her and gave her a peck on her check. 'Good. I don't think you'll regret it. It'll give you a chance to see more of France while you're here. And I know my mother will be pleased to meet you. And, of course, I'd love you to stay too. Now, please pack up your things, and we'll leave in about ten minutes.'

Looking up into his steady eyes, she felt he was speaking the truth.

The only worry she had at the back of her mind was that she was becoming more attached to Jon. Would she suffer when it was time to say goodbye to him? Could she go back to her previous life in Highminster without feeling bereft without him? Was she just going to make her life more miserable in the future?

No doubt she would be learning more about him and his background, and possibly his girlfriends, when she went home with him — and met his mother. It would be interesting — but would it also be agonizing? She feared it would be when her love affair in France was finally over.

'Hurry up, we have a train to catch!' His words as he left broke into her thoughts, and her need to prepare for the journey made her concentrate on the task at hand.

They left the hotel promptly and took a taxi — because Jon couldn't manage to drive — to the railway station. He explained, 'I would like to have driven you to Provence today, but my arm isn't up to it.'

There was still a slightly stilted air between them, as if their squabble had somehow resulted in a rift that hadn't entirely healed. Had the closeness they'd known gone forever?

Hazel sat opposite to him in the train carriage, aware of the other passengers around them, feeling remorseful. It was her fault after all. So she must try and repair it.

'Does your mother live in France?' she asked.

'She does indeed.'

'So she'll be pleased to see you while you are over here?'

He nodded. 'And to see you too.' He'd bought himself a newspaper, as well as a women's magazine for her to look at, and now began to read it.

Why does his mother want to see me? There was a lot she didn't understand — but she decided to let time go by and see what happened.

Jon dozed a great deal on the journey, though he took her for lunch in the dining car and made some polite conversation. However, she was quite glad of the restful time to doze herself, and to stare out of the window at the beautiful French countryside.

He'd told her that they were going to the South of France. Hazel was interested to hear him talk about the region, but he didn't say much. And her Geography lessons at school hadn't covered it. It would be all new for her to see and learn about — and that thrilled her.

At times, when she was staring out of the window as the train clanked along over the rail tracks, she suddenly became aware of him looking steadfastly at her. After a brief smile, he looked away. Was he wondering about her, as she was wondering about him?

She longed to break down the barrier that had formed between them.

Arriving at the Provence station where they disembarked, Jon helped her off the train. It surprised her to find stormy weather, not the sun the South of France was famous for. Where was the intense blue sky and warm sunshine? The palm tree fronds were sweeping frantically in the gusts of wind.

He remarked, 'Tut! Just our luck — a Mistral has come early this year!'

He ushered her into the railway station, and sat her down on one of the hard benches. 'I won't be long,' he said, and strode off.

Hazel looked around at the deserted station, and began to think it strange that there were no people about. 'Where is everyone?' she asked when he came back.

'Unfortunately, I didn't check the weather forecast before we came. There is a mighty wind outside — the locals call it a Mistral — it strikes this part of the world occasionally. And, just as I was about to show you the glories of Provence, we are caught in this storm.'

'Oh,' Hazel said weakly, 'what a shame.'

'Yes, it is. I've spoken to the station master who tells me it is a severe wind — unusual, in that the storms generally come later in the year, and are not as bad . . . I've phoned Mama, and she advises us to wait in town for a bit until the wind dies down before we climb the mountain roads.'

He certainly wasn't making it up about the wind, which almost blew Hazel off her feet as they were taken by a local taxi to a nearby hotel.

There was a gritty sandiness in the air too, which Jon explained came from the Sahara and was blown across the Rhone region during a Mistral gale.

The hotel was nothing like as grand and luxurious as the one they had left that morning in Paris. But it was clean and comfortable and they had a room each.

Hazel noticed the staff seemed to know Jon, and observed that he appeared not only to be willingly served, but actually liked, by them. Well, she reasoned, if his mother lived nearby, they were bound to know him.

'The locals reckon this storm will last another day at least,' he announced as he brought over some drinks for them. She noticed he hadn't asked her what she wanted, but the hotel had made the effort to provide her with a rather strange-looking pot with leaves in it.

Seeing her suspicious look at the pot, he suddenly laughed. 'It's French tea,' he said.

'Well, it's wet and warm.' Hazel chuckled too, wondering where the jug of milk was.

'As you can see out of the window, we're stuck here until tomorrow, and maybe the next day too. It's impossible for you to get home before the weekend.'

He picked up his *aperitif*, sipped it appreciatively; and, smacking his lips gently, he continued, 'To make this enforced stop worthwhile, I've been thinking that we might go down the road to the shopping centre and get you a sketchbook and crayons. Then you can make some sketches to take home with you to use as outlines to paint some pictures. We could find you somewhere out of the wind I'm sure where you could do some drawing.'

Hazel was thrilled with that idea and said so.

'I'm sorry to be costing you more and more money,' she said, thinking how all her savings would be swallowed up paying him back.

'Hazel, you will get a generous allowance from the government for assisting me in arresting those art thieves — '

'What do you mean? I didn't do anything — except perhaps make things more difficult for you.'

'Not true. If you hadn't found the guns, we couldn't have used them to confront and delay those slippery-fingered thieves disguised as workmen, then the police couldn't have overpowered them.'

Drinking her strange tea, which she found wasn't at all bad — refreshing, in fact — Hazel asked, 'What were all those weapons doing up in the attic?'

'They were stored there by Resistance fighters originally. At the end of the war, I daresay the guns that weren't used were forgotten about. They should have been handed in to the police, but it's likely the old couple downstairs forgot about them.'

Hazel said, 'I don't think I told you that I thought I saw someone in our bedroom at night. I didn't get the opportunity to ask Susan if she saw anyone — but then, she was a little the worse for drink, and probably slept too soundly.'

Jon licked his sore lip. 'Ah. That is easily explained. I asked the old couple downstairs to keep an eye on you two girls. I should imagine the little caretaker downstairs got her husband to go up and check up on you — make sure you were all right, as I paid them to.'

'But why would he go to the wardrobe?'

Jon lifted an eyebrow. 'Boyfriends can hide in wardrobes.'

Hazel laughed. 'So when you and Steve turned up, she sent for the police.'

'Exactly.'

They laughed.

However, Jon was showing his arm ached. He'd had to use it a bit to help move their luggage during the journey, and had gallantly assisted her on and off the train. His face was a little drawn, too.

'I'm tired, Jon,' she said, for his sake. 'Shall we have an early night?'

Hazel was aware that he received some ribald comments from the staff as they split up and retired to their separate bedrooms. In some ways, she was glad for the two rooms, as he needed rest as much as she did after their long journey from Paris. But in another way . . . indeed, she would have liked at least a prolonged goodnight kiss.

★　★　★

The following morning, a late, leisurely breakfast started the day as Hazel looked out of the window of the hotel to see the trees being battered by the still-very-windy weather.

'We're going to be held up here in the town for a bit longer,' Jon informed her gloomily.

She avoided remarking that perhaps she should be heading home, because she had already made up her mind to stay. And what difference would one day make to her already illicit absence from work?

'Let's make the best of it,' remarked Jon. 'Mama won't expect us until tomorrow now. I'm sure a stroll down into the town will be of interest to you.'

It was a battle to walk down to the shops in the still-blustery weather. Jon escorted her to a café.

They were enjoying delicious coffee and a gateau when a stunningly beautiful young lady burst into the café and looked around as if searching for someone.

When her eyes alighted on Jon, she looked pleased and moved towards him. Seeing her bearing down on him, Jon rose politely. It was clear to Hazel that he recognized her. It was natural for Jon to kiss her — that was what the French often did on meeting friends or family. After the greeting, she sat at the table, and looked coolly at Hazel when they were introduced.

After Jon had ordered some coffee for her, she began to talk to him most urgently in French.

Hazel thought she was rather rude, but she didn't know what they were discussing — and it might have been about something or someone she wouldn't have known anyway. But it seemed to Hazel that the French girl claimed his attention for far too long, and ignored Hazel's attempts to smile and be friendly.

Celeste — that was her name — gabbled away in French, although Jon tried to translate for Hazel so that she was not entirely left out of the conversation. Nevertheless, it seemed clear to Hazel that this young lady wanted Jon entirely for herself.

Perhaps she was his girlfriend? She certainly treated Jon as if he was

— although, for some reason, Hazel thought Jon was not as keen on her as she was on him.

Hazel decided, watching them, that as Jon's relatives lived in this part of France, he was bound to know many people — however, she couldn't dismiss from her mind that Celeste had probably heard that he'd come into town, and had been searching for him.

When at last Jon turned to Hazel and suggested, rather firmly, that they went and got on with their shopping, Celeste looked far from pleased as they said their goodbyes.

Hazel wondered if Celeste didn't have anything better to do than chat all day. But, she thought, maybe she was being unfair to Jon's elegant French girlfriend — the Mistral wind might be preventing her from working.

Jon escorted Hazel to pay the bill, explaining quietly, 'Celeste is an old childhood friend. She has just been though a very painful divorce, I gather — and she is, I think, hoping I'm still available.'

'Are you?'

He winked at her. 'We'll see.'

'I don't think she's your type.'

He said in a teasing voice, 'Are you feeling a wee bit jealous, Hazel?'

The fact that she was made her blush, but fortunately she didn't have to answer, because he had opened the street door for her and they were out on the windy street again.

He escorted her to a shop that sold art materials, and made sure she bought a sketchbook and pencils. 'You can do some sketching,' he told her.

Then he took her to *La Perfumier*. 'To buy some perfume for your mother,' he suggested, after she'd been tempted to acquire one or two items for herself — the shopkeeper was a very good saleswoman and the French packaging was so pretty.

Hazel asked, 'What about something nice for *your* mother?'

'Oh, I have something very, very special for her,' he replied.

He was obviously very fond of his

mother, and Hazel was pleased, although she wondered what she was like and how she would get on with her.

During the rest of the day, Hazel managed to get a few sketches made in her new sketchbook: one in the ancient church; and one where they stopped for lunch, looking out of the café window. And one she made of Jon, while he read a newspaper. Whether he knew she was sketching him, she wasn't sure. Or did he think she was drawing the rather disgruntled dog lying nearby while his owner was dining? Hazel was sure the poor dog would have liked a walk rather than being sat there.

The day slipped by, and Jon told her the weather was easing and that he hoped they would be able to get up the mountain to see his mother in the morning.

'I feel I might be able to drive tomorrow,' Jon told her, 'my arm is easing.'

'I'm pleased to hear you're feeling a lot better,' she said sincerely.

9

Jon hired a Citroën car to take them up to the chateau.

The sun hadn't yet come out to shine brilliantly over the landscape as it usually did. His arm was still sore, and driving a challenge for him, so he wrestled with his concentration, and was conscientious with the steering wheel, as he was keen to avoid an accident. He steered the car most carefully, as the road was bumpy in places; and, the higher they got, the more dangerous a fall off the road could be.

But, as he drove up the road that was familiar to him, he was also thinking about Hazel.

He'd got to know Hazel very well during the past week, and felt sure she was the girl for him. But did she feel the same? Could she feel the same attachment to him when she met and learned about his family and background? He would have to see.

That was why he had decided to take her to meet his mother — for Hazel to learn about his French ancestors and relations. It would be one thing to tell her, quite another for her to actually see the situation for herself. Then she could decide if she wanted to deepen their relationship.

So far, they had been thrown together by circumstances. The next step was for her to choose to be with him.

A quick glance at her showed him that she was staring out of the passenger window, completely absorbed in the panoramic view of the Provence countryside. No doubt it was her artistic nature that was making her admire the view that had captured her attention, so he didn't have to talk to her, and could examine his position.

He was aware that his security work could put him in possible danger, which had been his decision. He'd thought, at the end of the war, it was his duty to do something worthwhile to help France to get on its feet again. And so he had been assigned to assist the Art Recovery Department.

However, he had no right to involve Hazel in any possible danger. That presented a problem for him. He could cope — defend himself and shoot a thief — but Hazel couldn't. She'd gallantly helped him a few days ago, but she wouldn't want to be worried in the future about him being a target for villains.

He gripped the steering wheel tightly at the thought of her being vulnerable, until the twinge of pain in his arm told him to take the pressure off.

He could tell her, in all honesty, that the likelihood of either of them being involved in that kind of trouble in England was remote. In London, maybe, but in rural Highminster, where most of the population had no knowledge of art — or wanted to — they might have heard of the Mona Lisa, but that would be the extent of their interest!

Before he'd met Hazel, Jon had decided to work and settle down in England and buy a home there. Soon his work in France would be finished.

Not that Jon was in any way torn because of his dual nationality — why should he be? He loved both countries.

When the Germans had invaded France, his parents had sent him to England to be with his maternal grandparents. He was educated there. But he served with the Free French Army, as did his father — who, sadly, had been killed fighting.

Recently, he'd given serious thought to getting married — after the only girl he'd proposed to had refused! Now the picture was different. He definitely had Hazel in mind.

Would Hazel fit into his life? Would she agree to marry him and accept the possibility of any danger to him — or her? Perhaps she would prefer to marry an Englishman. A plain, ordinary Englishman, with no foreign strings attached. He would just have to see.

*　*　*

Hazel didn't tell him that she was more than a little nervous of the drive up the mountain. It wasn't that she didn't trust his driving — it was heights she didn't like. Walking on the rooftops of Paris hadn't cured her vertigo! The road seemed to be on the very edge of the mountain at times; it made her shiver with fright as she imagined the car toppling over it.

Jon remarked, 'Shame the weather isn't a bit better, you'd get a magnificent view from here on a nice day.'

'How much further?' was all she could say.

'Here we are. The sun has come out to greet us.'

They had arrived at a village, a pretty place that Hazel's artistic eye could see was very paintable. Cottages with colourful flowers, that grew not only in pots but also seemed to be wild.

Two women with shopping baskets, who had obviously stopped for a chat, noticed the car driving past and waved to Jon.

When he turned into a drive with some large ornate gates, Hazel could see a beautifully-proportioned eighteenth-century house ahead of them. 'My goodness.' She blinked, agog. 'Don't tell me your mother lives *here*?'

'She does. Do you mind?'

'Why should I mind? In fact, I think it looks a really lovely French chateau.'

'Good. I hope you're going to like her too — '

'I'm sure I will.'

He drove the car around to the side of the house, past trimmed shrubs, and into a big cobbled yard that had been built for horses and carriages years ago. Here, they were greeted by a man in overalls washing a stately-looking car.

The excited conversation in French that went on between the men enabled

Hazel to get out to stretch her legs, and gaze around the old stables. Without knowing much French — although she felt she was learning it quickly, and remembering more from her school days — she understood that Jon was being greeted warmly.

An old dog lumbered up to him, wagging its tail. Jon bent down to stroke it. There were hens, ducks and geese wandering around, too.

She studied Jon, knowing that he felt at home from his broad grin and animated conversation.

'Come along in,' he said, coming to join her and showing her towards a side door. He'd left their luggage for the man to bring in, although Hazel carried her handbag.

As Hazel walked into the chateau, many questions came into her mind. Was this charming old French house where Jon's mother lived? Did she own it?

Hazel pondered what Jon had told her. Was she right in thinking this was where Jon was bought up as a young child, until the Germans invaded France and he was evacuated to England?

Their footsteps echoed on the marble floors, and Hazel's eyes were darting here and there, viewing the charming French décor.

Soon a plump woman in an overall appeared and waddled towards them. She greeted Jon with a hug and a kiss, and an outpouring of speech, which he translated for Hazel: 'My mother has gone into the village to visit a sick child — but she is expected back soon. Shall we go into the saloon and wait for her?'

Hazel was shown into a gracious room, rich with eighteenth-century furnishings. She admired the design of the high ceiling and the long windows, woodcarvings and carpets. It was as if she'd walked into a museum of valuable works of art, and it took her breath away as she looked around.

Coffee was brought in for them on a tray.

'Pour the coffee, will you please, Hazel?'

It amused Hazel to think of herself as the hostess and mistress of this elegant house as she poured the steaming drink from a silver pot and handed it to Jon, who'd slumped down on a chair and crossed his long legs as if he felt at home — and maybe he did?

She would have been bold enough to ask him, but as soon as he'd drunk his coffee, she had to get up and take his empty cup because he had fallen asleep.

After a short nap, he shook his head and, looking over at her, muttered, 'Sorry, I must have fallen asleep.'

'That's all right. You are still recovering from your injuries. The nap will have done you good.'

He beamed at her. 'Thanks for being so understanding, Hazel. I feel so relaxed with you, as if I haven't got to be on my best behaviour all the time.'

She wasn't sure if he meant she wasn't of any consequence, and therefore he didn't have to be polite all the time, or — and she hoped this was the case — he regarded her as a true friend, like a close relative he could be at home with, who wouldn't take offence at anything he did, within reason.

So she smiled back at him, saying, 'You go ahead and snooze. May I wander around and look at the furniture — you won't think I'm being nosey, will you? You know I like good craftsmanship and pictures.'

He waved his hand. 'Go ahead and look. I'll join you shortly.'

She didn't venture into the kitchen area, where she heard women talking and the clatter of plates, and from where a delicious smell wafted out. There was a vestibule by the front door with panelling and furniture to admire. Doors led to other rooms, but Hazel was loath to open them, and found enough to see in a drawing room with French tables and chairs, an ornate fireplace, and expensive carpets. She observed that some of the upholstery on the chairs was well-worn and needed reupholstering. She remembered her father telling her that houses needed constant attention as things wore out. And, looking at the walls, she noticed where some parts needed a lick of paint or a new piece of wallpaper inserting.

Jon caught up with her and escorted her to what Hazel thought was a small, comfortable sitting room for a lady. His hand took her arm towards a wall where she could see a blank space — but no, there were picture hooks where small pictures had been taken down.

Hazel guessed immediately why they were looking at the wall.

With her fingers over her mouth, she exclaimed, 'This is where the miniatures belong!'

'Yes, indeed. They are Mama's.'

Now she understood why Jon had been so keen to catch the thieves in Paris and acquire the stolen art.

He removed the small packages from his pocket and unwrapped the little paintings carefully. 'Come on, Hazel. Let's have yours.'

She'd almost forgotten that he'd given

her two which she'd placed in her hand-bag several days ago. She unwrapped them, hoping no harm had come to them, and was relieved that they were still in their original wrappings — safe and sound.

Hanging them back on the wall was a tense moment. It gave Hazel a thrill to see them on display back home — where they belonged — as Jon was trying to remember which one went in which position.

'I hope I've got them in the right places,' he said, standing back and admiring the collection.

Hazel stood admiring them: all portraits, some older than others. All presumably very valuable, as they were exquisitely painted.

'Come on,' Jon said, 'let me show you upstairs.'

Ascending the staircase, Jon said, 'Some Germans were here during part of the war, and a few of them bashed it about a bit, but we have repaired what we could.'

He didn't show her behind every door, but they climbed the stairs to a room that he told her used to be his nursery. He chatted about his childhood memories, making her laugh about the naughty things he'd got up to.

A clear English feminine voice sounded from below. 'Hello, come down! I want to see you.'

'That's Mama,' Jon said, leaving her and galloping down the stairs to greet his mother.

'Put me down, Jon!' She spoke to him in perfect English. The merry laughter made Hazel realize that he had taken his mother into his arms.

Coming downstairs herself, she saw a spritely, grey-haired lady holding onto Jon's hand. Hazel didn't have to be introduced — she knew it must be his mother looking up proudly at him.

'This is Hazel, the efficient secretary I told you about — '

His mother looked kindly at Hazel, saying, 'You forgot to mention how beautiful Miss Crick is.' She kissed Hazel on the cheek and made her feel at home immediately.

'Lunch is ready. A soup with some freshly made bread and cheeses I brought up from the village.'

Down to earth simplicity and a homely quality, in contrast with the grandeur of their surroundings, was what Hazel admired. His mother seemed to be able to combine the two and made her feel as if she was welcome.

Hazel was questioned about her home and job — all in a pleasant, friendly way.

His mother was anxious to know about what her son had been up to. 'I don't like to see you all bandaged up — and how is your arm you told me was injured?'

'It's a long story, Mama.'

His mother smiled at Hazel. 'I like long stories.'

Jon winked at Hazel. 'First may we have coffee served in your sitting room, Mama?'

His mother looked surprised. 'If you wish, dear, but we usually have coffee in the drawing room.'

Jon had risen to take back his mother's chair so that she could rise easily, then he did the same for Hazel.

'I have the feeling you two have a surprise for me?'

John and Hazel grinned at each other.

'Yes, you definitely have,' the old lady said as she walked towards the room.

At first his mother didn't notice anything as she walked in and seated herself in her favourite chair.

'I hope you are going to tell me that you've brought some perfume from Paris,' she said.

'Damn it, I forgot,' Jon said. 'I'll be sure to get you some for Christmas.'

When the coffee was brought in by the housekeeper and served, they sipped the hot liquid and sat saying nothing.

'Well now, please tell me about this mystery you've got up your sleeve, Jon.'

'You should have noticed it, Mama.'

He put down his coffee cup and walked over to the wall and stood by the miniatures.

His mother watched him and suddenly her hand went over her mouth — Hazel rose rapidly to take her coffee cup the old lady's hand and place it on the small table near her chair as she was in danger of spilling it.

'Jon — you found them!'

Then, to Hazel's dismay, Mama put down her coffee cup and began to weep.

Hazel ran to kneel by her chair, and put her arm around the lady.

Jon was alarmed to see his mother distressed when he had expected her to be overjoyed.

'Forgive me for being so emotional,' Mama said. 'I never thought I would see them again.' She found her prettily embroidered handkerchief and dabbed her eyes.

Her voice wobbled as she explained, 'They mean so much to me. My family portraits they are . . . and seeing my beloved husband again is . . . ' Too overwhelmed to say more, she sobbed again.

Hazel's sympathy made her swallow. Yes, indeed she knew what it was like to love a man now . . .

Then Mama rose slowly and went over to the wall to examine the pictures closely. She looked at each painting in turn and remarked, 'They're in perfect condition.' She turned to her son, whose embarrassment at his mother's reaction to what he'd imagined would delight her, made him appear uncomfortable.

'Where did you find them, Jon?'

He cleared his throat. 'You remember, Mama, when the war started and France was being occupied, Father joined the Free French Army. He didn't know whether there would be any fighting in this part of France, as it happened there wasn't. But he wanted to protect some of your treasured possessions, so he took these portraits which were easily carried, to Paris where they were put in a vault with other works of art for safekeeping.'

Mama nodded. 'Yes, your father knew it was not just the value of the paintings — for me they are valuable for being the only pictures I have of my father, mother, and husband, grandparents — and one that is of my brother, Rupert, who was killed at Dunkirk.'

She turned to look at Hazel with watery eyes. 'You see, my dear, my family house was bombed in London during the war. All my family things destroyed.'

What a tragedy! Hazel felt deeply for her. She understood how pictures, whether they were valuable or not, could be treasured by someone.

Mama gave her eyes another dab and returned to her chair. 'Jon, I do thank you. Now tell me how you found them.'

Jon went up to Hazel and kissed her cheek. 'You should thank this young lady too, Mama. Without her help I'd never have got them back for you.'

Hazel protested she had little to do with the recovery.

But when they were all seated again, he started to tell his mother about his work for the French Government overseeing the security of the works of art that were being returned to their owners — and combating art thieves who were trying to steal what they could.

'Small objects are easier for them to steal,' Jon said. 'I recognized these miniatures when saw them in the Louvre vault. And when I heard of them being targeted by a gang of thieves, I not only wanted to get hold of the pictures before they disappeared — I wanted to capture the thieves before they stole anything else. So I organized an operation to do just that.'

'And I almost wrecked it,' chipped in Hazel.

Jon gave a chuckle. 'You almost did — but then, with your help, the operation was successful.' He beamed at her and she gave him a wide smile back.

At Mama's request, they went on to

the talk about the whole saga — including Hazel being found in Jon's car and having to be brought to Paris, which made Mama laugh. The whole story from the start was interesting to Hazel too, as she had the opportunity to ask questions and fill in her knowledge about Jon's dangerous security work.

'Will you be continuing with that job in Paris?' she asked, anxious that she may not see him again.

'It's more or less over for me,' he replied.

'So you'll be working again in England?' She held her breath.

'That's the idea.'

Hazel wondered whether his mother would approve of him being in England, but she was told that Jon was free to choose what he did. Hazel was then surprised to hear her say, 'Your position as Count here, Jon, is only an old title. It gives you no privileges only responsibilities.'

Ah, thought Hazel, *that explains why I was told a Count had his room in*

Paris — he is a Count!

Mama assured him that she'd been looking after the chateau since his father had left home and would continue to do so. 'As long as you come to see me occasionally, Jon dear, I am happy to know you are doing a job you think is worthwhile. You can fly over here easily for holidays at any time.'

Dinner time came around quickly and they had to discuss the plans for the next day.

'I must get back to my job in England,' said Hazel. 'My boss, Mr. Payne, will be in a dreadful muddle without me to organize things for him.'

So it was decided that Jon and Hazel would get up early the following morning and fly from a nearby airfield to England.

Jon went off to book the tickets while Hazel and his mother chatted.

'I'm so glad Jon met you,' the Comtesse said.

'As I am, to have met you, and Jon.'

There were words and feelings left

unexpressed between them, but before they could say any more, their communication was interrupted by Jon, who charged into the room saying, 'Celeste has arrived. She asks for my help, urgently. Anyway, she's very upset, so I'd better go and see what's wrong.'

'Yes, of course, you must go and help her,' his mother agreed.

It was, Hazel thought, kind of his mother to send him to help someone in need when she would probably be thinking it was a shame she saw so little of her son and would have preferred him to have stayed with her that evening.

That was certainly the way Hazel thought.

When Jon had hurried away with Celeste — and Hazel was glad Jon hadn't brought her in — she thought of something that might please the Countess. Taking her handbag, Hazel took out her sketchbook and showed her the sketch of Jon she'd made in the café.

'Oh, Hazel — what a clever artist you

are — you've caught him exactly.'

Hazel felt a little unsure as she asked, 'Would you like it?'

'My dear, indeed I would!' Her eyes sparkled with delight. 'I'll get a frame made and it and will go with my other miniatures.'

Flattered to think of her art with such exalted work, Hazel blushed. But then she remembered what Jon's mother had said about the miniatures — she valued them not because they were priceless works of art — but because she loved the people in the portraits and they were all precious for her. Jon too had known that and had gone to tremendous lengths to get them back for his mother.

'I think you have drawn this sketch of Jon with a loving hand.'

Hazel blushed and to hide her embarrassment — was it obvious she loved him?

Not long after Jon departed, the ladies enjoyed their evening meal together. Hazel learned more about

Jon's ancestry and his inheritance.

They were having their dessert when the Countess said, 'It is such a shame Jon has been called away. He should be back by now.'

Hazel longed to question her about Celeste, but didn't want to appear inquisitive.

It was unfortunate that she'd fallen in love with a French aristocrat. Plain Mr. Hunter was a possible man for her to aspire to — someone of his status was quite out of the question. But she lapped up all the information his mother told her about him.

As the hours went by and Jon hadn't returned, his mother suggested they should both retire, and Hazel agreed. She was shown into a pretty, comfortable guest bedroom — but it had none of the modern amenities like an ensuite.

She lay in bed thinking about Celeste. Was she a bit of a drama queen? Was she trying to seduce Jon, now that her marriage had ended? She knew Jon had certain duties to fulfil as a land owner. He was a capable young man, well able to sort out problems when he could. He was dependable, although could be too domineering . . .

Jon's mother hadn't said a word against Celeste — but neither had she said anything which showed she thought highly of the young lady.

In the morning, Hazel was told that Jon had phoned late last night to say he was very sorry but he couldn't come to England with Hazel. He was tied up with Celeste's problems — which annoyed Hazel intensely. He left a message to say a taxi would collect her and would take her to the airport, where her flight ticket would be waiting for her.

He was very sorry to have to leave her to travel back to England by herself — but he didn't go on and explain why he wouldn't come too.

Hiding her annoyance not to be told the reason, she tried to seem cheerful and positive about the way she'd been left to fend for herself. Her newly acquired sense of independence, and knowledge of French, as well as knowing she had enough money to make the journey home quite comfortably, helped her to accept the disappointment.

The Countess was kindness itself and said she was sure Jon would have a good reason to have to stay behind, but Hazel detected that she too didn't like the situation, and would have liked her son to have stayed with them that evening, and tomorrow to taken Hazel back to England.

'My dear Hazel, it has been a delight for me to have you here,' the lady said, when they both retired. 'Your bravery assisting Jon to acquire my miniatures has earned you a place here — come any time you like.'

It was heartfelt, Hazel knew, and she thanked her, regretting that although she would love to come again — it was not going to be possible — highly unlikely.

The following morning a taxi took her to the airport early. As it was a small airport she didn't have to wait long to get through customs and get on board.

All the time, before she left France, Hazel looked out to see if by any chance Jon had come to see her off — but, much to her disappointment, he didn't appear.

Celeste was obviously more important to him.

10

A dreary grey, wet day greeted Hazel on her arrival in England. Yet colourful autumnal leaves were falling and being blown about in the wind — but with nothing like the strength of the Mistral wind in France she thought.

Her journey from France had been uneventful, everything Hazel felt she could take in her stride. She was, she realized, now a more mature woman than when she been a frightened girl leaving England for the first time a week ago.

It was late afternoon by the time she clicked open the garden gate and walked towards her parents front door — much too late to go to college and explain her absence to Mr. Payne.

Opening the front door with her key, she heard the anxious call from the kitchen, 'Who's there?'

'Me, of course, Mum.'

Hugs and kisses from her mother made Hazel feel at home and despite all the wonderful places she'd visited, and awesome experiences she had in the last few days, home she felt was definitely where she was glad to be.

'Dad's in the garden sweeping up the leaves, Hazel. Go and fetch him while I put the kettle on, then we can sit down and hear all about your adventures.'

There was no point in telling her Mum everything that had happened to her. Hazel made light of the train of events that she'd been through — ignoring the unpleasant bits — so that her parents could enjoy the tale and think that all their worrying about her had been unnecessary.

'You haven't told us much about Jon Hunter,' her father observed.

'I thought I'd told you rather a lot. What else would you like to know?'

Mum looked at Dad and smiled.

She wasn't going to tell them that she'd fallen in love with him — or that his station in life made him out of reach for her.

'Look, Mr. Hunter took me to Paris because he had to — I've explained why. I was able to help him with a job he was doing there.' Hazel didn't want to elaborate on the frightening aspects of what she'd been through. 'It was wonderful having the opportunity of seeing the Paris sights. The art in the Louvre Museum — what I saw of it, stunned me. I would love to go to there again. The only reason I couldn't come back earlier was because of the Mistral wind — you have no idea how strong that wind was.'

'Is Mr. Hunter returning to do his job here?'

'He told me he was going to.'

Mum said, 'So you'll be seeing him again?'

'I expect so.'

'He has a lovely voice, Hazel. He sounded like he cared about you, yet you don't sound as if you care much about him — '

Hazel almost lost her temper. 'Of course I care about him! He gave me every help — as I told you. He even took me and Susan to the famous Moulin Rouge music hall one evening, which would have cost him a pretty penny.'

Dad grunted. 'Seems to me as though he has plenty of pennies!'

Hazel couldn't bear hearing any criticism of Jon. It hurt her to have his kindness dismissed, so before her parents could question her further about him and the huge expense she'd cost him, she asked, 'Did Mr. Payne get in touch with you?'

Her father replied, 'Yes, he did. He seems a fussy man.'

Hazel looked concerned, saying, 'Yes he is I suppose. Mr. Payne likes things done properly.' She sighed. 'There's a lot of paperwork involved running a college — especially at the beginning of the college year.'

'That's what he said, Hazel. He told me he was going to hire a temporary secretary to get on with your work.'

Hazel made a face. But what else could she expect? She'd been away for practically a week and she was sure her In Tray would have been overflowing. 'I'll go in early tomorrow morning and sort things out,' she told her parents.

★   ★   ★

When morning came Hazel tried to slip out of the house quietly without disturbing her parents. Outside the sun hadn't fully risen and it seemed chilly so she wrapped her scarf around her neck and stamped her feet to keep them warm while she waited for the bus to take her into town.

The usual crowd she met in the mornings were not on this bus because she was catching one earlier than the one she usually caught.

Time to reflect on what she was going to say to Mr. Payne, she made up her mind to be honest about her absence from work. She would promise to put in some extra hours to catch up on anything he wanted done.

When she walked into her office she was surprised to see a plump girl already seated at her desk.

'Hello,' Hazel said pleasantly.

The girl's glasses shone at Hazel as she looked a little harassed and snapped, 'I can't help you at the moment — look at this muddle the last secretary left behind.' She ran her fingers over some sheets and sighed saying, 'I came in early because I'm trying to sort this muddle out.'

Hazel gaped. It did appear as though a puppy had got up on her desk and enjoyed itself scattering the papers about. She said, 'I certainly didn't leave a clutter like this when I left work last Friday — everything was up-to-date and in order.'

The girl batted her long eyelashes as she gave Hazel a challenging smile. 'Well, if you're the girl who was here before me, your idea of order isn't mine! Mr. Payne has asked me to reorganize the files in this office — '

Irritated, Hazel said, 'Leave it to me. I'll soon get it back tidily as it was.' She moved as if she wanted the girl to get up from her desk chair, but the girl didn't move.

With a frown Hazel said firmly, 'I'm Hazel Crick, Mr. Payne's secretary, and I'd like you to allow me to sit at *my desk* and get on with *my work*.'

'Excuse me, Miss Crick, you *were* Mr. Payne's secretary I believe. I'm Miss Grayson. I was sent here from the Highminster Office Staff Agency last week. I've been appointed by Mr. Payne to take over as his secretary, as from yesterday.' She didn't add, *so there* — but that is what it seemed like to Hazel.

'Well,' muttered Hazel, 'we'll see about that!' However, she realized that it wasn't this new girl's fault if she'd been told to fill in for her. And, in a way it wasn't the principal's fault either as he'd needed a replacement for her quickly.

Afraid she might say more than she

should, Hazel said no more. She looked at her untidy desk, and the young secretary behind it, and almost laughed. What fastidious Mr. Payne would make of Miss Grayson's help she didn't like to think — but the thought occurred to her that the more the girl got her filing system in a mess the more Hazel would have to clear up. So she made a great sigh of regret and walked out of the room and headed for the principal's office.

As she approached Mr. Payne's office she found him walking towards her from the opposite end of the corridor. 'Good morning, Miss Crick,' he called. She thought he didn't seem too pleased to see her.

He walked into his office and held the door open for Hazel to come in too.

Taking off his coat and hat which he put in a cupboard he remarked, 'Did you enjoy your jaunt to Paris?'

Taken by surprise, Hazel blinked. 'It wasn't exactly a jaunt for me you know, Mr. Payne.'

He sat down at his desk and indicated that she should sit opposite him. He picked up some papers and his fountain pen from his inside jacket pocket as if he was waiting to begin his day's work.

'I'm sorry I was delayed in France,' began Hazel, 'but I came here early to try and catch up but I found Miss Grayson in my office.'

'That's right. Miss Grayson has taken over from you as my personal secretary.'

Hazel's mouth opened in astonishment before her outburst, 'Why? Mr. Payne, I've only been away for a few days!'

He fiddled with his pen, and said, 'Absent without leave.'

'But, but, you must understand I was taken to France against my will.'

He replied dryly, 'From what Mr. Hunter told me over the phone, he was giving you the chance to see the sights of Paris.'

Hazel couldn't deny that was true. She asked, 'Didn't he mention that I was helping the French police catch some art thieves?'

'No, Miss Crick, he did not. He may have mentioned it to your parents. But whatever you were up to is not my concern. I am, as you know, having a lot of work to do. I couldn't sit around and wait for you to finish your holiday I had to get a temporary typist in to do your work.'

'Yes, yes, I can understand that — but have you seen the way my files have been tossed around? Chaos it is. Miss Grayson hasn't a clue how to do the job.'

Mr. Payne sighed, and gave Hazel a weak smile. 'Miss Crick, that chaos as you call it was not caused by Miss Grayson, but by a girl from the typing pool they sent to me temporarily. Miss Grayson has only just come, yesterday afternoon. She is as well qualified as you and will be able to reorganize things — now, I really must get on . . . '

What could Hazel do? The decision

had been made to replace her.

Hazel rose as if in a dream. As she walked toward the door, Mr. Payne called out, 'I'll give you a first-class reference.'

Hazel didn't reply.

She'd been given the sack! She hadn't any money coming in any more. Her plans to save for a home of her own were in shreds. Tears welled in her eyes.

She walked slowly down the corridor unsure of what to do. Ahead of her was the student's café, so she walked in and went to get herself a cup of coffee.

As it was so noisy and crowded with young students no one took any notice of her. There were some students sitting alone and reading while they had their breakfast coffee, so Hazel on her own was not noticed.

She couldn't really blame anyone for her misfortune. But it hurt her. She would have to sign on at the Employment Exchange and search for another job.

The coffee tasted awful after the French coffee she'd been enjoying.

Her eyes were suddenly drawn towards the door where the tall figure of Jon Hunter was standing looking around as though he was searching for someone.

When his eyes alighted on her they softened.

Several of the female students watched him walk like a panther through the room to where she was sitting.

Without saying anything he bent and kissed her on both cheeks.

Flattered the man the girls were eyeing had chosen to come to her — and the French habit of kissing someone on both cheeks had been bestowed on her — Hazel smiled. 'Hello Jon.'

'I went to look for you in your office — '

'I've been given the sack.'

He looked stunned. It made her realize he had nothing to do with it.

'Why?'

'Absent without leave, Mr. Payne told me.'

He plonked himself down beside her and put his large warm hand on hers.

'I'm truly sorry,' he said, and looking into his clear blue eyes for a moment or two, she could see he was sympathetic. 'You didn't deserve that.'

'Mr. Payne told me he would give me a good reference,' she sniffed as tears threatened.

'Mmm. That doesn't exactly cover the blow, does it?'

Being honest with him, she shook her head. 'No.'

'We must talk this over. Would you like another drink?'

She swallowed. 'Yes please. But don't buy the coffee — it's awful here.'

He grinned. 'I always drink tea in England.' He marched off and returned with two cups of tea.

After taking a sip of tea — she always liked to watch his lips as he drank — he said, 'I have to explain about Celeste.'

She almost retorted, *I don't care about the wretched woman.*

But of course she did.

'I think I should tell you, Hazel. Otherwise you may be wondering why I didn't come back to England with you.'

He went on to tell her how he'd known Celeste since they were children. 'Until I was sent to school in England we were like brother and sister — she grew up to be a very beautiful lady, as you saw.'

Hazel recalled the chic young woman — and her look of disdain for her. If she was close to Jon in the past she probably saw her as a rival, especially as Jon had said her marriage was not a success and she knew Jon was available.

He twirled the tea leaves in his cup and she thought he was feeling embarrassed as if he was making a confession. 'When I was younger, I asked her to marry me. But she chose someone else — although I warned her about him . . . consequently, when things went wrong for her I wasn't surprised — although I was sorry.'

'How very sad!' Hazel wasn't curious to ask about the divorce but he didn't seem to want to tell her.

After a pause, as if he was trying to

push it out of his mind too, he said, 'That's partly why I decided to take a job in England — to be away from her. Although I'm fond of Celeste, I'll never marry her — '

'Why not?'

'Because I've fallen in love with another girl.'

'Oh!' Hazel wasn't surprised, with his looks and money he would attract many women.

Jon cupped his large hand over hers and was looking at her with a serious expression on his face. 'Don't you want to know who has captured my heart?'

Certain it would be a French girl, Hazel shook her fair hair. She stared down into her teacup leaves. She was wondering if her future could be seen there. Her fortune shown in the tea leaves.

He removed his hand from hers and looked up at the ceiling. Perhaps she'd hurt his pride by showing so definitely that she wasn't interested in his love life.

Hazel took a deep breath, and changed the subject. 'Were you able to help Celeste yesterday?'

He breathed deeply. 'I hope so. She has to face the future, decide what to do with her life — she's got a lot going for her and shouldn't be feeling sorry for herself. Or angling after me. There are lots of things she could do. I'm hoping my mother will take her in hand, make her see the possibilities she has in life. Help her to find something she enjoys doing.'

Hazel felt that the same applied to her. It was not the end of her life just because she'd lost her job. She would search for another, but today she needed to get over the shock. Get away from the college. 'Look, the students have gone off to their classes,' Hazel remarked, looking around at the now empty chairs and tables, and the cleaner going around tidying up the café.

Guessing she didn't want to talk with the clatter of china being collected on trays and tables being wiped, Jon suggested they walk in the park.

'Don't you have to go to work?' she asked as they strolled outside.

He grinned. 'I'm the boss. I have taken some holiday time off.'

The sun had come out and the fiery reds, yellows and copper-coloured wet leaves made her wish she had her paints with her. Earthy smells and flowering shrubs provided added pleasure to enjoying her walk in the park with Jon.

They laughed as two young squirrels frolicked in the sunshine and leapt about the trees.

'Hazel, tell me, have you any plans now?'

She shuffled her feet through a pile of fallen leaves. 'I haven't had a chance to think what I could do — except sign on as unemployed.' She gave a bitter little laugh.

'You could work for me.'

'Really?' She stopped walking and turned to look up at his face to see if he was being serious. 'Are you seriously offering me a job?'

'Why shouldn't I? You're a first-class secretary and I could do with one. You can start immediately as I do have a lot of paperwork to catch up with. I have to find a house to live in too — and you could help with that, couldn't you?'

It all sounded very exciting, very convenient too. 'I'll take it,' she said.

'Brilliant! I'll tell you about my job here — what I do — and how you can help me.'

*   *   *

By the end of the week Hazel was installed in a bare Nissen hut, which was Jon's temporary office while the grand local government building was being built. She was thrown into a busy schedule with many things to learn and files of the paperwork to make. Answering the phone and even the tea making she was expected to do. Then there were meetings that Jon wished her to attend to make notes so she had to quickly brush up on her shorthand.

She didn't see much of Jon most days. He was out and about seeing to his responsibilities first hand. Hazel got the impression that not only was he good at his job, he enjoyed it too.

Occasionally he went house hunting for himself and took Hazel with him. As he explained she would be able to point out things that a woman noticed she liked or disliked — besides, a second opinion of a house was useful.

Hazel enjoyed working for him. She found the work absorbing. Her hours were similar to the college hours she'd had, and as Jon picked her up outside the college gates each day and dropped her in the evening by the bus stop where she was used to catching the bus home — the move of job made little difference to her. And he paid her the same as the college had done.

'You're always talking about Jon Hunter, Hazel,' her mother said one evening. 'When are we going to meet him?'

Hazel shrugged pretending she didn't

mind whether they did or they didn't see him. To tell the truth she was acutely aware of her parents' ordinary home, compared with Jon's mother's chateau. Not that she thought Jon would make her parents uncomfortable or boast about his aristocratic upbringing — it was just that she loved him and she didn't want him to feel uncomfortable in her homely English home. Although she felt sure the digs he was living in at present were no different. But then, he was looking for a house and that would definitely be an up market family home like several he'd taken her out to see already.

Mum said, 'It's your birthday next week. Why don't you ask him over for a meal after work?'

Hazel agreed she would ask, but she told them she had no idea about what he did in his private life and he may well already have his evenings booked.

She worried about asking him. Would her parents ply him with questions? And even worse, hint he was courting her? It would be so embarrassing — she decided not to ask him home. Make excuses.

★   ★   ★

Hazel was delighted to receive a phone call one day from Susan, the little air hostess.

'I'm in England for a few days next month, Hazel. How about us meeting?'

That idea delighted Hazel. 'Yes, I'd love to see you again, Susan. Only I can't get away from work — I'm working for Jon now.'

A giggle came from the other end of the phone. 'That doesn't surprise me one bit, Hazel. I always told you he'd got his eye on you — '

'We're not having an affair, Susan!'

'I didn't say you were. I only said — '

'You thought he was sweet on me — just because he spent a fortune on me in France.'

'So he did — that was because he likes you.'

Hazel laughed, 'OK, OK you win. I like him and he likes me. But he's the boss and I'm only one of his employees, and I can't take the day off and come up to London, much as I'd like to see you.'

'Don't worry, I'll come to Highminster for the day.'

'That would be lovely having a day to enjoy together! The weather is quite balmy for the time of the year — but rain is never far away.'

'I'm coming to see *you*, and chat to *you*, Hazel! I don't care about the weather forecast.'

Hazel was sure Susan would do most of the chatting as she was so good at it — and chuckled. 'Even if it's raining, we could meet up at the lunch hour and after work for a few hours. Let me know which day you plan to come. Bye.'

When she told Jon about Susan's call, he appeared to be pleased she'd kept in touch. He suggested the day she came Hazel could leave work so that the girls could both go out together for most of the day.

'Thanks, Jon. I know Susan would like it if you joined us for lunch at a pub.'

'I don't see why not — as long as you don't feel I'm gate-crashing.'

Hazel smiled. She wanted to tell him that nothing would please her more than his company. And she knew Susan liked him too.

11

A big surprise awaited Hazel a day later.

Jon drove her into a garage one morning.

She thought he'd gone for petrol and when she was told to hop out of the car, she wondered if he'd got a problem with the car that needed seeing to.

'Come with me,' he said striding off towards the garage office. Here he was met by a suited salesman, who beamed at them.

'I have two to show you, Mr. Hunter,' said the salesman. 'Shall we show the lady, and she can decide which one she'd like?'

Thinking they were talking about some other lady than herself, Hazel trotted along with them to view two small cars parked side by side on the forecourt.

'Which car would you like, Hazel?'

She took it to mean: which car do you prefer? Just as she was asked about the houses she was viewing with him. He seemed to value her opinion — if she said the kitchen was too small for example or pointed out that the view over the cemetery wasn't ideal. So she said, 'I really don't know anything about cars — I can't even drive.'

Jon said nonchalantly, 'Driving lessons will be thrown in. So which colour do you prefer?'

'I think they are both nice. I like the red one and the blue one.'

He seemed to become a little bored, as if he wanted to get back work. Then domineering when he snapped, 'Miss Crick, please will you make up your mind which one of these cars you'd like.'

She chuckled. 'It doesn't matter — I haven't a garage either.'

'Cars don't have to be garaged.'

This conversation was becoming ridiculous but Hazel was enjoying it.

'I'm a secretary, not a chauffeur.'

Jon breathed a long sigh and said, 'Come and sit in this one.' He had opened the door of one of the cars and indicated that she sit in it.

'Why?' she asked, suddenly cross.

'Because I'm going to buy it for you, Hazel!'

She gasped as he went on, 'It's a birthday present. You won't have to catch the bus to work and will be free to drive around to the shops — and even take your parents out for a run.'

'How did you know it was my birthday?'

The salesman, realizing this young couple needed privacy to sort out their affairs, left them and returned to his office.

Jon replied to her question, 'I know it's your birthday, in the same way you told me you knew my personal information — I read your file when I took you on as an employee.'

'But . . . but, Jon this is way out of line for a *birthday present*. I can't afford to run a car anyway.'

He kicked a stone across the gravel. 'You won't have to worry. I will own the car, think of it as a company car, and I'll maintain it for you.'

Excitement rose in Hazel as her eyes widened. It was not just the thrill of having a car, but the sheer kindness of him. He didn't have to do this for her. My goodness, a simple bunch of flowers would have been enough and would have pleased her.

'You have left me speechless,' she said.

'Well, for goodness sake hurry up and decide which one you want.' He looked at his watch. 'I have a meeting to go to shortly.'

'Amazing!' was all Hazel could think of to say.

They were being watched by the salesman from his glass-fronted office. He returned when he observed their tiff was over, and delighted they'd decided to buy one of the cars, he invited them into his office to sign the papers.

It was later that day after Hazel had had her first driving lesson that she began to regret having been so dismissive in showing him that she didn't care about his love life. Because she did. It was becoming clear to her now that he really did think highly of her. Maybe he really did love her — as she did him? It was not as impossible as she'd always imagined it was because of the social divide between them. Since the war it didn't seem to matter anymore who your parents were or how rich they were. Young people made their own lives which was liberating — a challenge — especially for women working just as she was doing.

Working with him was a joy. His interests were largely hers. They both liked the outdoor life as well as Art, and now that he was visiting houses with a view to finding a home for himself she found she liked similar things.

Hazel, she said to herself — *you've been an idiot!*

Every morning she loved to see his car coming to pick her up, his welcoming smile. Once seated in the passenger seat, she had the urge to bend sidewards to kiss him. She liked to watch his strong hands on the steering wheel and wanted to run her fingers over them. His voice was a comfort to hear, so strong, and he always had something positive or amusing to say. She looked forward to hearing what they were going to be doing each day — even if it was a day in the office preferably with him around.

Idiot or not, she had to cast her personal feelings aside as she worked with him — fortunately there was so much to occupy her mind with the various projects he was involved in.

Anyway, the thought of having a little car to buzz around by herself was exciting. That meant she had to work hard at learning to drive and reading the Highway Code.

★ ★ ★

Jon Hunter — the Comte de la Fare — was not a quitter. He was disturbed by Hazel showing little sign of wanting to know anything about his private life or to become attached to him. He felt they were made for each other as the saying goes. It was clear to him the moment he'd first set eyes on her — despite the icy reception he'd got when she told him in no uncertain terms that he had to put the bloody posters up himself!

He'd liked her looks as well as her personality.

He was also impressed to find that when she was up against trouble she was brave. Walking along the rooftops of Paris was no mean feat. Shivering down in the sewers of Paris would have made most girls scream — but not his Hazel. She did her very best to help him with his operation.

His mama liked Hazel too. He'd been shown the little portrait she'd made of him — his mother loved it quite as much as her other treasured miniatures.

Yes, Hazel had come into his life and enriched it.

And he didn't want to lose her.

Being half French he had a romantic soul. Everything to a Frenchman was an art: the art of cooking; the art of painting; the art of making love.

These skills had to be acquired. They couldn't be rushed. He would have to persuade Hazel that his love for her was genuine.

But how? That was his problem. He was her employer and wouldn't take advantage of that situation. Jon was aware that his position as a French count, and his training as an officer, had given him a confidence that some would call arrogance. And he had to admit he had to control his natural ability to want to command a situation. But that wouldn't work with asking a girl to marry him. Indeed it wouldn't work with Hazel. She had to decide for herself whether she wanted to marry him. And as he had already told her Celeste had turned him down . . . his chances with Hazel seemed dicey.

He would just have to wait and hope

the right situation would come along soon and Hazel might — he hoped she would — become as enchanted by him, as he was with her.

* ★ *

When Susan's visit loomed Jon suggested the day she came to Highminster, Hazel could practise her driving and take Susan out in her little car with her L plates on before meeting him at a restaurant for lunch.

Hazel decided she'd like to show Susan the small manor house at Wentworth before they went to eat. She'd liked the house and wanted to know what Susan thought of it. It was an old manor house, and had been cleverly modernized to suit people who liked to live in comfort and good design. Double glazing was coming on the market which did not spoil the mullion windows but kept the draughts out. An Aga cooker provided the big kitchen with constant warmth and hot water. Ideal for working folk to come home to at the end of a busy day. Plenty of room, both inside and outside the house for children's play areas . . . all these thoughts were going through Hazel's head as she viewed the property. The garden almost came into the house through a new conservatory so anyone could wander out to see the well-kept mature trees and shrubs.

It was much too big for Jon to live in alone, but a great family home she hoped it would become for him one day.

★   ★   ★

Busy and enjoying his job, Jon was unaware that the art thieves who had been caught in Paris belonged to a larger international group. After their plot to steal the miniatures had been foiled, they were keeping their eyes open for where the little paintings had got to. They had buyers abroad who'd offered them a huge price — and they didn't want to lose the sale. So they were searching to snatch them back.

Fortunately, they didn't know that Jon had given them back to his mother in Provence. But they did learn that Jon, the security man who'd cleverly changed the miniature packets for packets of sand in the cigarette packets, was in England — but didn't know where, until chatty little Susan mentioned in a London pub that that she was going to Highminster to see Jon Hunter — and the girl who'd helped him save the miniatures in Paris.

Susan's lively story was overheard by a member of the underworld who listened in pubs to collect payment for selling any information to the criminals.

When the art thieves heard about Jon Hunter's whereabouts they set about a plan to recover the miniatures. These criminals had no qualms about harming anyone in their quest to steal anything they wanted to sell on to art collectors.

Had Jon, or the security department he'd worked for, had known of this, they would have immediately arranged for Jon and Hazel to have bodyguards. But they did not.

*   *   *

The morning Susan arrived in High-minster it was a fine early winter day. The trees now almost bare of leaves and stood out like skeletons in the sky. But the stillness of the landscape hid the wildlife searching for food. The low temperature made the threat of snow possible — but rain was more possible.

Susan bounced off the train and almost ran to meet waiting Hazel.

With excited voices the two girls exchanged hugs and pleasantries.

'Thanks for coming. Lovely to see you again, Susan.'

Susan was not short of conversation of course, and soon they were chatting about many topics, including Hazel going missing in Paris, and her discovering the attic ammunition store.

'I missed all the fun,' declared Susan.

'No, you didn't — I assure you it

wasn't fun balancing on the roof top and being stuck down a sewer for hours!'

Hazel steered her friend towards the best tea shop in town and they sat chatting while they had refreshments.

They seemed to have so much to talk about, but Hazel glanced at her watch. 'I want to take you to see a manor house now before lunch. It's one that Jon may buy — '

'For you both?'

Hazel shook her head vehemently. 'Don't be silly, Susan. For him — and maybe for his girlfriend too. I don't know.'

Susan looked at Hazel and blinked. 'Has he got a girlfriend — a special one, I mean?'

'Dunno.'

'Really Hazel, for an intelligent girl, you surprise me. You have one glaring fault — you seem to be blind at times. You have a habit of jumping to conclusions, with no evidence at all.'

'What do you mean?'

'I remember you were dead certain

the Jon had turned down your painting for the art exhibition at Highminster, and he hadn't, had he? Now you are certain he has a girlfriend, and you don't know who she is, or anything about her. Does she exist — or is she just in your imagination?'

Susan's remark jolted Hazel. She said defensively, 'I don't interfere with Jon's private life. I'm just his secretary remember.'

Susan made a face as she raised her eyebrows, but Hazel ignored her. 'Anyway,' Hazel continued, 'he's going to meet us at a restaurant for lunch, so we'd better get going to have the time to see a manor just outside Wentworth first. I think he's thinking of buying it. He'll be glad of your opinion I'm sure. I'm going to drive you there, Susan — I hope you don't mind me driving you?'

Susan looked surprised. 'Why should I mind?'

'Because, I'm still learning to drive.'

Susan smiled. 'We all had to learn . . .' She proceeded to relate all the amusing incidents that had occurred when she was learning to drive.

Proudly Hazel sat Susan in the passenger seat of her new car. She deliberately told her that it was an office car — not hers — and that Jon had provided it for her to do her job.

Being driven didn't stop Susan's flow of conversation and the two girls set off along the country lanes chatting and laughing — but Hazel kept a close eye on the road. Wet leaves on the roads could be slippery at times.

Out in the countryside Hazel relaxed as there were fewer cars, traffic lights and pedestrian crossings to worry about.

What neither she nor Susan expected was that a car parked on the other side of the road facing them would suddenly pull out in front of them.

'Look out! That idiot is coming straight at us!' yelled Susan putting out her hand to grasp the steering wheel to make the car swerve away.

It was too late to avoid a crash — an ear-splitting noise shook the girls rigid.

Hazel's little car tottered on two wheels for a few seconds ... then it plunged off the road and slowly rolled into the roadside ditch.

Susan screamed. The jolt and sudden pain winded Hazel.

The two men who came to help the girls out of the car were far from being gentle rescuers.

It was obvious that Hazel had been hurt — she was unconscious. Blood was oozing from a head wound and running down her dazed face.

Susan in the passenger seat — although screaming — was soon quietened by a sharp slap on the face by an ugly-lookinging man. 'Shut up!' he snarled. Susan was savagely hauled out of the car and up onto the edge of the road where the car that had crashed into them was alongside with other men inside it.

A weasel-like lad took Susan's jaw and spat at her saying, 'That's the dame who knows where Mr. Jonathan Hunter is.'

Susan was amazed. Still shaking from

the accident, she said, 'Please help my friend, she's been hurt.'

'Lady, we're not here to help anybody.'

That was clear and there was nothing Susan could do to help her friend as she was dragged towards the car that was waiting with its engine running, and pushed in the back seat where there was another man with a gun pointed at her.

'What are you doing? I can't leave Hazel. She needs medical attention.'

'You'll need some soon, if you don't do as you're told. You're coming with us to the village phone box to ring Mr. Hunter and tell him to come immediately. Tell him we're here to collect the miniatures he stole from us.'

Susan was frightened — but as an air hostess she'd been trained in emergency procedures. *Keep calm* she told herself. *These oafs won't get the better of Jon Hunter. It's just stupid of them to think Jon is going to give them back his mother's miniatures. But I must warn him that Hazel needs help and that he is in danger.*

How can I do that? Susan wondered in trepidation as she was being held uncomfortably tight. Whisked away from the accident in the villains' car towards the village she had noticed the sign, Wentworth, by the side of the road.

In the village, which was peaceful and had a large village pond, the car came to a screeching halt by the side of the phone box.

Susan was grasped and shoved into the box together with one of kidnappers.

The man grabbed the receiver and thrust it into her hands. 'Ring Hunter and tell him to come here *now*.' She was given a scrap of paper with a phone number on it. 'This is his office number.' She could feel the barrel of the pistol he held prodding into her back.

Quickly thinking, Susan took a deep breath to steady her nerves and phoned the police instead with a shaky hand.

'Constable Thorne speaking. Can I help?'

Keeping as calm as she was able to, Susan replied, 'Yes, please. There has been a fatal accident on the road out of Highminster. Tell Mr. Jon Hunter he must come immediately to . . . What's the name of this village?' she asked.

When the man opened the phone box door to ask his fellow criminals the name of the village, Susan quickly added, 'Constable, this is an emergency. Warn Jon Hunter on his hotline that armed men have kidnapped us, Hazel Crick and Susan Marshall. Tell him . . .' She went on softly, and speaking in French, *'Je suis serieux. Tres dangerous. Criminels avec un revolver —*'

That was all Susan was able to say in French before she had to say that the village she'd been told was Wentworth. Then the phone receiver was snatched from her hand.

Susan just prayed that she'd said enough to warn Jon.

'Let me get back to look after my friend who's been hurt,' she begged. When the villains seemed unsure whether to let her go, Susan said promptly, 'Any motorist coming along the road will see there's been an accident and will call for the police and an ambulance.'

With their faces together the thugs decided to let Susan go, as they planned to ambush Jon.

Not offering her a lift, poor Susan had to walk back to where Hazel lay by the side of the road, hoping her friend was not badly hurt.

★   ★   ★

Jon was surprised when Hazel and Susan didn't turn up at the restaurant as they had arranged. He kept glancing at his watch. As the time went by he began to think he should find out why they hadn't come to meet him as arranged. He kept telling himself that there could be any amount of reasons — but surely they should have phoned the pub and let him know they weren't coming?

Disappointed, he drove back to his

office and waited by the phone.

Prowling around the empty desk where Hazel usually sat, he found he couldn't concentrate and get on with his day's work. Other members of his staff soon realized he was out of sorts and stayed out of his way. He managed to spill the milk making himself a cup of tea Hazel usually made for him. He knew he was on edge. He kept trying to keep the worst of his fears at bay.

Finally he rushed to the phone and rang Hazel's home.

'Good afternoon, Mr. Crick, it's Mr. Hunter speaking. Can you tell me where Hazel is please?'

'Oh, hello, Mr. Hunter. No, I'm afraid I can't. I thought she'd gone off to work as usual and planned to meet a friend at lunchtime — isn't she there?'

Controlling a twinge of annoyance, Jon answered, 'She didn't turn up at the restaurant where we had planned to meet for lunch.'

'Oh dear! I'll ask the wife, perhaps she'll know.'

Jon could hear Molly being called and after a minute or two he heard the rather breathless female voice say, 'Mr. Hunter, I'm sorry I don't know where Hazel could be — she told me she was going to meet the friend she went to France with, who was visiting Highminster today. It's a cold day and looks as if it will pour with rain at any moment — I was going to hang my washing out but — '

'Thank you, Mrs. Crick.' Jon was conscious of being rude interrupting her but he was more concerned to find out quickly where Hazel was — what could have happened to her, and Susan.

'Let me know if you hear anything — or if she turns up, will you?'

He made sure she had his office phone number and abruptly put the receiver down. Where on earth was Hazel?

He recalled Hazel had particularly liked the house they both viewed at Wentworth. Maybe she'd gone there to view it with Susan? Although he would have thought she would have told him.

Besides, she would have to collect the keys from the estate agent so that was unlikely. But she *could* have gone to get them and asked to be shown around the property again — it all took time. Was that why the girls were late meeting him?

Jon decided she may have been cross with him because he'd rushed her through the house, and hadn't said he wanted it — maybe she was becoming tired of him not making up his mind where he wanted to live.

Perhaps he'd misunderstood what they had arranged? Did he ask her to meet him at the manor house instead of the restaurant — and he'd forgotten? Were the girls waiting for him to get there?

He decided he would drive over to Wentworth and see if he could find them. He picked up his coat because the weather had changed. Mrs. Crick was right, the heavens looked as if they were about to open.

The phone rang as he was about to

leave his office. He decided to leave it to one of his staff to answer but he was called as he fitted his hat on his head.

'Mr. Hunter! There's an urgent message for you — '

Blast it! He didn't want to be held back — but he did return to answer the phone.

It was the police saying he had to ring his contact at the security department — urgently.

Which he did.

'Hello, Mr. Hunter, sir. A strange message has just been received for you.'

Jon groaned. He could have done without strange messages at this time. But when the message was relayed to him he gripped the phone tightly.

'Sir, we can't make much sense of it — it's partly in French — can you understand it?'

'Yes,' Jon replied. '*It is* an emergency. Inform the chief constable to ring me *now*. And get an ambulance to deal with an accident on the road to Wentworth, someone has been gravely injured.'

He slammed down the receiver.

Jon was panting as he waited for the phone to ring again. Which it did almost immediately, and he was able to discuss quickly with the chief constable how they were going to deal with a ruthless pack of thieves on a revenge mission to obtain his mother's little paintings.

'I'll send some armed officers and meet you there, sir.'

Jon also made sure he had his pistol with him before he left his office.

12

The rain started thundering on the roof of his car as Jon drove out of town towards the village of Wentworth. That noise meant nothing to him, only the pounding of his heart and the fear of what he might find occupied his mind.

He'd recognized Susan's warning in the phone message, and had been deeply shocked. The fact that she'd sent it partly in French told him it was what he feared, that the art thieves were after him — and the miniatures. They had somehow found out where he was in England, and were probably going to blackmail him by threatening to hurt the girls if he didn't hand the miniatures they wanted to them.

Hazel had been injured, badly, if she needed an ambulance. Susan, who had kept her wits, was vulnerable.

He knew he must have those evil

men rounded up and put away in jail. His mama might be in danger if they were able to discover where the miniatures were.

These thieves were the worst kind. They obviously had a market lined up for the little paintings and when they were taken by him, they were probably furious to have lost the sale. Stealing was their way of life. They didn't want to get the reputation in their trade that they were unreliable. They had to find the miniatures and dispatch anyone who thwarted them.

Jon's job was to catch them.

Somehow.

He was sure the police and ambulance would turn up. What worried him stiff was the state Hazel was in — how badly hurt was she?

His conscience smote him too. Had he allowed Hazel to become a victim of the thieves by accepting her help to obtain his mother's valuable miniatures in Paris? The miniatures were valuable, but a drop in the ocean compared with some of the priceless works of art he'd been guarding while they had been transported back to their museums and private owners. It was only because they belonged to his family that he'd been so keen to acquire them.

He knew he was dealing with vengeful thugs. They had abused him once — he didn't look forward to having to fight them again.

The sooner they were locked away the better.

Knowing the countryside around Highminster well, he decided not to take the road directly to Wentworth where he might be expected by the villains who probably lay in wait to ambush him. He took a narrow winding road there, via farms, with high hedges on either side, hoping he didn't meet a herd of cows going to be milked — or a tractor which might block his way for ages.

He felt unsure of how he was going to deal with the situation.

He was one of perhaps two, three or four of them. He was a crack shot, but they would have weapons too. The only comfort he could think of was that often these criminals were not as bright as they thought they were. They hadn't considered that both Susan and he spoke French — he was sure they didn't, as they had allowed Susan to give him the message of warning.

He slowed down as he approached a T junction and a signpost pointing to the village from the side road.

Suddenly he saw a small figure sitting by the side of the road at the road junction.

Cricky! Who on earth was that? Some child playing? But he could see no other children about, besides it was raining and why would they sit down and get soaked?

Cautiously he edged nearer in his car.

It was Susan sitting there!

She looked up and recognized him at the same time. Standing, she ran towards him as he got out of his car.

'Jon!' she cried, flinging her arms around him — he could see she was very agitated — dripping wet and sobbing. 'I, I had to leave Hazel. They made me go the village to telephone you. I was trying to get back to her . . . but I can't walk anymore, the heel's come off my shoe.'

'Where's Hazel?' He tried to ignore the fact she was making him all wet.

Susan pointed in the direction she was going. 'They let me go back to her.' She gulped. 'But I had to walk miles.'

Jon thought that was a mistake they'd made — they could have kept Susan as a hostage. They obviously didn't realize Susan had warned him, which gave him confidence.

'Let's get you in my car. You can direct me to where Hazel is — '

'Take care, Jon! They're horrible men. They're waiting to harm you.'

'How many are there, Susan?' He grabbed the car rug from the back seat to cover her.

'I saw four.'

'The police will be going to the village to capture them. In the meantime keep your head down, Susan, then no one will be able to take a pot shot at you if any villains are about.'

Susan sat in the passenger seat of his car trying to explain what had happened, how the criminals' car had deliberately rammed them. Jon listened but tried to concentrate on what awaited him as he drove his car cautiously towards the scene of the accident. His whole attention was given to what he was about to see.

For a moment or two he felt numb when he found Hazel's car where it had gone off the road and was now lodged on its side in a muddy ditch. Pulling up to see if anyone was around, he gripped the steering wheel and peered over it, his eyes searching, until he gasped in horror — it was Hazel's body he saw!

He shut his eyes, breathing in little gasps. Was Hazel alive?

'Stay here!' he ordered Susan as he got out of his car with his revolver ready to use. Ignoring the beating rain, he moved to examine the stricken car — praying that Hazel had not been killed!

He discovered Hazel's body slumped forward, her forehead bleeding, unconscious in the driver's seat.

He slid down the bank and opened the car door, easing her body towards him. She was breathing still, but how badly injured she was he couldn't tell.

She was saying some words that Jon couldn't understand. He stroked her, reassuring her as he was trying to think what to do.

Except, pray.

Suddenly, the sound of the ambulance's siren could be heard in the distance. Very soon it became louder as the vehicle approached — its flashing lights almost blinding him.

The ambulance crew were magnificent. Used to dealing with car accidents, they took over and Jon could only admire their expertise.

'There's another young lady in my car, who was in the accident. Would you take a look at her?'

Going back up to his car, he opened the car door and the ambulance men assisted Susan into the ambulance.

'Can you tell me if the girl's injuries are serious?'

The ambulance man shook his head. 'Afraid we can't, sir. A doctor will have to decide — you'll have to come to the hospital to find out.'

Thankful at least the girls were in safe hands, Jon breathed more freely. He wanted to go with the girls to hospital — he couldn't. He had the criminals to think about — some unfinished work to do.

He saw the ambulance turn around and watched it until it become smaller as it headed off towards Highminster — with his love in it. He sighed.

'Now for the heavies.' He shook himself and clambered back into his car. Making a neat three-point turn, he faced the village of Wentworth leaving his pistol handy on the passenger seat beside him.

Crawling along the village street at about twenty miles an hour, he saw nothing unusual. Until he spied a police car and parked his car beside it.

Picking up his gun, he got out of his car, keeping his eyes moving for any sign of activity. There was none he could see. Coming into the centre by the village church, it struck him that it was odd no one was about.

'Stay where you are!' He was confronted by a policeman brandishing a baton.

Jon fished his security badge out of his pocket to show the policeman.

'Where are the thieves we're after?'

The policeman pointed towards the telephone box and said, 'Over there, sir. We've got them surrounded.'

Jon grimaced. 'Not caught yet?'

'No, sir. They are wandering about. Difficult for us to round them up because they are armed — and we're not.'

They were joined by a senior officer. Jon told him that he would go to the pub and phone the number of the village phone box. He would tell the thieves that he would meet them at the church with the miniatures, this would mean that all four criminals would get in their car and he could confront them with his gun and then the police would be able to swoop on them more easily.

'Dangerous for you, Mr. Hunter.'

'Dangerous, possibly — but necessary,' Jon replied. He was prepared to take the risk of being shot at. His main concern was to get the arrest over quickly and get back to the hospital to see how Hazel was.

Giving the criminals time to think he'd gone to collect the miniatures, Jon stood amongst the gravestones in the village churchyard. He had to make sure the thieves saw him, but as the villains' car approached, he hoped standing there as if for target practice, he would not be shot at.

The armed police acted fast though, and as the thieves got out of their car searching for Jon, they were overpowered before they got close to him.

Jon had crouched down amongst the gravestones taking cover, hearing shouting and some gunfire. After a few anxious minutes he thanked his lucky stars he was still alive.

* * *

Later, in the accident department of the hospital, Jon soon found Susan who told him that she was OK and that the medical staff had carted Hazel away on a trolley for an assessment.

Jon told her that the criminals had been captured.

Susan was pleased to hear about that. Then she said, 'I really need to buy a pair of shoes, before I leave for London. And a new outfit — mine would not pass inspection. An air hostess should always look spick and span.'

Jon chuckled at her determination to enjoy a bit of shopping — get something positive out of her trip to Highminster.

They agreed to go into town, have a late lunch and visit a department store and a shoe shop.

Jon didn't have to keep his mind on

what they ate and drank at the pub, or to take much notice as Susan tried on endless pairs of shoes until she decided on the pair she liked. Waiting for her to decide on a new costume could have been a pain, only her constant chatter — all of it light-hearted — was soothing for Jon as a background to his main thoughts which were on Hazel.

She didn't mind at all when he offered to pay for her shopping.

Putting her on the train back to London, he thanked her. Susan said, 'Ring me and let me know how Hazel is, will you?' The train, with a puff of steam, was chugging out of the station as she leant out of the window waving and called to him, 'Now go and buy an engagement ring!'

*   *   *

Back in the hospital Jon waited anxiously in the bleak waiting room, pacing up and down, until he was told that Hazel wasn't badly injured and he was able to phone her parents and tell them.

A doctor came to see Jon and explained that although they could find no major injury, Hazel ought to remain in hospital for several hours because she had knocked her head and that could be serious.

'Don't worry,' the doctor reassured him. 'You may go and see her now. I expect she'll be allowed home by the end of the day — you must just make sure she is kept quiet — you'll have to look after her — get her a light supper.'

The doctor obviously thought he was her husband and he wished he was.

Shortly afterwards a nurse came and showed him which room Hazel been taken to.

'Don't stay long. She needs to rest,' the nurse instructed him as she opened the door to see the patient.

Hazel was propped up in a hospital bed, looking exhausted with a bandaged head.

Her eyes had purple rims. 'Sorry, Jon,'

she said on recognising him, 'I must have slipped off the road. The other car came straight at me. I'm afraid your car is smashed up.'

He gave her a fond smile that brought a slight smile on her face. He said, after he'd kissed her pale cheek, 'I'm pleased to see you're in one piece — I don't care about the car.'

'I do. I love my little car.'

'I'm sure the garage will patch it up as the nurses have patched you up. Are you in pain?'

'Only from feeling what a clot I am. I was listening to Susan chatting, and driving far too fast on that country road I expect. I wanted to take Susan to look over the Wentworth Manor House, that I'm sure is just right for you, before we met you at the pub. I think it's a lovely house and hope she'd think so too — and encourage you to buy it.'

'I may,' he interrupted her because he felt she was talking too much.

But Hazel went on, 'Anyway, when that car came at me suddenly, I wasn't experienced enough to avoid the crash, I swerved, and toppled over into the ditch.'

Jon pressed his lips together. 'It wasn't your fault. They rammed you on purpose. Susan told me. I'll explain why that happened, but not now.'

'I don't think I'll be able to drive ever again.'

'Of course you will.'

Jon understood her temporary loss of confidence in her ability to drive. He knew she was a good driver and would just need some encouragement to get going again. He said, 'I told your parents that you've had a knock and asked them to put a hot water bottle in your bed — the doctor expects you to be discharged from hospital this evening. Then, he told me, you must take it easy.'

He sat by her bed and held her hand, she smiled contentedly and didn't attempt to pull it away.

'I'll be alright soon, Jon. It was such a nasty shock. I feel as if I'm all black and blue.'

Then no more as she'd fallen asleep.

He rang his garage asking them to collect Hazel's car and repair it. He also rang his office to make sure his office staff knew what was expected of them, so that he didn't have to return that day and would be taking some time off tomorrow, because Hazel had met with an accident.

Jon wanted to take Hazel home as it would be easier for him than for her elderly parents to fetch her. Besides, he wanted to meet them. Assure them that their daughter could have as much time off work as she needed to fully recover.

13

Next day Hazel woke up refreshed. For a moment or two she couldn't work out why she was still in bed when her bedside clock told her that it was two in the afternoon.

Must get a new battery for that clock, she thought, turning over to snuggle down again.

Ouch! Pain made her realize why she in bed. Or was she dreaming that something like a steamroller had rolled over her?

A noise at the door made her pull down the bedclothes to see her mother coming in with a tray — and the cat, who nimbly jumped up on her bed, and purred as she put out her hand to stroke the furry animal.

'How are you feeling, Hazel?'

'Sore, Mum, very sore.'

Her mother fussed over the pillows

behind her as she got her daughter to sit up to eat the egg and cress sandwiches she'd made for her and poured her out a cup of tea.

'Was Mr. Hunter very cross with me smashing up his car?' Hazel asked.

Her mum chuckled. 'I think you'd have to do worse than that to make him find fault with you, dear. He's besotted with you.'

Hazel smiled. 'Yes, he is kind. A very kind man.'

Hazel's mother sat on the side of the bed and said, 'Your father and I like him very much. We thought it was nice of him to bring you home and help you upstairs for us yesterday. He said he'd call in later on this evening and see how you are.'

Hazel smiled broadly. 'Can you give him something to eat? He's bound to be hungry after work.'

Nodding, Mum said, 'I've some stew left over from lunch, I'll warm that up for him.'

'Mum, you can't offer him leftover

stew — he's a French Count!'

'Is he now? Well, I can't offer him frogs' legs or snails from the garden, if that's what he's used to.'

Hazel giggled. 'Your stew is always very tasty, Mum. Dad could dig some new potatoes from his vegetable patch and some runner beans if there are any left. And would you make an apple pie? Your apple pies are delicious. And ask Dad to nip round to the corner shop and buy a threepenny carton of cream to go with it.'

'He'll have to make do with custard.'

Hazel lay back. 'The French drink wine with their meals,' she said.

'The English don't, and he's half English he's told us.'

Hazel sipped the last of her cup of tea. 'I know. But the aristocracy in England have wine with their dinner too I should think.'

'Here, give me your cup before you spill the dregs. Mr. Hunter told me he was sent to school here when the war started. His maternal grandparents lived in a Birmingham suburb, and he attended a grammar school there as a boy when he was evacuated during the war. Nothing fancy by the sound of it.'

Hazel had presumed — quite wrongly — that Jon's grandparents lived in some grand hall or mansion. Not, as was the truth of it, an ordinary English suburban house. *How wrong can you be? she asked herself.* Susan is right, I do jump to conclusions.

Curious, she asked, 'How did his mother come to marry a French Count?'

'I'm surprised you haven't asked him that question.'

There was a tap in the bedroom door. Jon poked his head around the door he'd opened a bit. 'Couldn't help overhearing . . . '

He shifted himself into the room. 'May I come in?'

'You are in by the look of it, Mr. Hunter,' remarked Mrs. Crick. 'I'll leave you to chat to Hazel. Only for a short time mind — don't tire her out.' She picked up the tray and Jon opened the door wide for her to leave. Before she left them she asked Jon, 'We were wondering if you would like some stew for your supper tonight?'

'Mmm . . . lovely! A home-cooked meal is always a treat for me.'

'There you are, Hazel. The way to a man's heart is through his stomach!'

Hazel blushed as Jon closed the door after her mum, and he came towards her with a bunch of flowers in his hand.

'Mum can be rather forthright at times,' she remarked. 'Are these for me? How kind of you, Jon. I love roses.'

Jon grinned at her. 'The way to a woman's heart is by giving her a dozen red roses — so they say.'

Hazel giggled. She was flattered — yet anxious. Embarrassed — had her mother hinted that she was planning to inveigle him into marriage?

'My English grandmother was a nurse during the First World War.'

He'd sat himself down on the bedroom chair and placed the bunch of flowers on the bed beside her — and the cat who'd curled up by her.

'My grandfather was a wounded French soldier, he came to England to convalesce — that's how they met.'

'Oh.'

'He just happened to be a French aristocrat. Like me.'

Hazel looked down at her flowers and fingered the soft petals of one rose. She didn't know what to say.

But Jon chuckled. 'One doesn't choose one's parents. It made little impression on me that his ancestors escaped the guillotine! I just admired and loved them. My father was the best of fathers, and I regret I saw so little of him before he decided to fight for his country and was killed.'

'I'm sorry for you,' murmured Hazel, imagining how awful it would have been for him to lose his beloved father when he was young. And for his mama to lose her husband too.

But Jon was more concerned to talk about her. 'I've been told not to overtire you — and this is certainly not the time to discuss things like why you wanted to see the house at Wentworth again — I'll give you time to recover from your ordeal first.'

It was a relief to her that he had, in his usual dominant way, told her she must wait, giving her the time to absorb the information that had changed her perspective of him. She now knew that although he was an aristocrat on his father's side, his mother had been a working woman — a nurse. It explained why his mother spoke English so well and he was equally at home in England and France.

However, a gloom descended like a thick fog over her, as she began thinking of his girlfriend, Celeste. Perhaps she was more exhausted after the accident than she'd thought.

He went on the tell her that her car was on the road again — nothing seriously wrong was found with it. 'You must drive it as soon as you can — it's like falling off a horse, Hazel. It takes courage to mount again. But you need to drive and forget the bump you've had. Put it down to experience.'

Hazel could see the sense of that, her earlier reluctance forgotten. 'Of course I'll drive again. I've enjoyed having the little car — '

'And other things I hope you will soon have,' Jon said, rising. 'I'm going to leave you before your mum tells me off.'

'Enjoy Mum's meal,' she called to him after he'd kissed her on the cheek and strode over to the door.

He stopped and turned to say, 'I'm looking forward to it. And to seeing you tomorrow, Hazel. We have a lot of important things to discuss. I'll pick you up at say, six o'clock, after I've finished work?'

Hazel stared at the closed door after he'd gone. What important things did he want to discuss with her? Surely any work-related topic could wait until she was back in the office? Perhaps he was going to buy Wentworth Manor after all. Was his wedding due soon?

In the late morning next day, the doctor popped in to see how Hazel was.

'She's on the mend,' he informed her parents. 'We always have to be careful with a patient who has suffered a head injury. Make sure she takes it easy for a while. Ring me if she says she's suffering from a severe headache.'

Hazel however felt fine. 'You really don't need to treat me like a piece of fragile china, Mum. I'm enjoying being at home today with you and Dad — and the prospect of a night out with Jon is something I'm looking forward to very much.'

Mum looked at Dad and winked.

She had the luxury of an electric fire put in her room, so that she could prepare for the evening in a leisurely fashion.

She wore the simple yet chic dress she'd bought in Paris, clipped on the necklace Jon had given her, and liberally sprayed herself with the toilet water he'd chosen for her.

'How beautiful you look,' her mother

said when she arrived downstairs. 'Dad, come and look at your daughter.'

Her father was clearly proud of his daughter and kissed her saying, 'Mind you enjoy yourself, m'dear.'

Jon arrived at promptly six o'clock, all nicely showered, casually, but smartly dressed, and with a broad smile. With warnings that sounded a bit like the fairy godmother's advice to Cinderella not to be too late home, Hazel and Jon set off.

'Does it bother you to be going to Wentworth, Hazel? Along the same road where you had your accident?'

'It does, and it doesn't,' she told him. 'For one thing I'm not driving . . . ' She could have added: 'And I'm with you and you make me feel protected — safe.'

Their first stop was an upmarket pub, near Wentworth, where they enjoyed a drink and a plate of fish and chips — well-cooked as Hazel liked it to be. The blazing fire in the old chimney fireplace was cosy — typically English, as was the background murmur of drinkers' voices and occasional laughter.

'Please stop asking me how I feel, Jon. I'm fine — and enjoying myself.'

'Being here? Or, being with me?'

'Both.'

'That's a good start.'

Hazel looked at him quizzically. 'Start to what?'

'The evening.'

Hazel's mouth went up at the corners as her eyes caught his. 'Remember what my parents told us — don't be back too late.'

'Right,' he said, fishing in his jacket pocket for his wallet, ready to walk over to the bar to pay the bill, 'we'd better get on then — the noise level has risen as many drinkers have come in, and we can hardly converse.'

'Where are we going?' Hazel wanted to know when they were installed in his car once more.

'Wentworth manor.'

'It seems a strange time of the day to

be viewing property. We won't see much in the dark.' What she wondered was as they were in the vicinity, maybe they could see it in a different light.

Once there, and walking outside in the fresh cold air, she asked him, 'Are you really interested in buying this manor, Jon?'

'If you like it.'

She breathed in deeply and said as she exhaled, 'Yes, I like the house — very much.'

'Enough to want to live in it?'

She remained silent. Then what she truly thought blurted out. 'Of course it's far too big for one person, Jon. But I expect you'll be marrying soon. It would suit a big family beautifully.' Then she shut up because she supposed he was thinking of getting married — soon?

Then she was thunderstruck. Was it *her* he had in mind? She had been so sure that there was another girl, and as Susan had told her, this imaginary woman didn't exist! She had just about swallowed this awesome truth when Jon said, 'You haven't asked me: what's the point in going there at this time of night?'

She laughed. 'Go on then, tell me.'

'I've something to show you — something I don't think you've seen.'

Curious, she said, 'I don't think there's anything I haven't seen there — '

'Wait and see.'

The manor house appealed to Hazel even in the semi-darkness of the moon-lit evening. A sense of tranquillity filled the air and made her breathe slowly as her eyes viewed the ancient building that seemed to grow up from where it stood, and had stood for centuries. Peaceful and right in its setting, with leafless oak and beech trees growing around it, looking as if they belonged there too.

Jon didn't steer her towards the house. He ushered her round the side of the house to look at the view over the garden and countryside beyond.

The stars were like silver pin pricks in the darkened sky, the moon a shining orb. The quietness gave time for reflection, while woodpigeons and rooks glided about the sky on their way to nest for the night. An owl, hooting, added to the scene.

Now Hazel understood why Jon wanted for her to see the manor in the moonlight. The view over the valley in front of them was spectacular and could have been missed by any prospective buyer in a hurry to see the house during the day.

Jon gently took her elbow and said in her ear, 'I want to ask you something.'

'Go ahead.'

Jon took a deep breath. 'Will you marry me?'

Her heart leapt, was she really hearing what she feared she would never hear? It was magical.

Without hesitation she replied, 'What about the girl you told me you had fallen in love with?'

Hazel turned to look at him. He went to lean back against an oak tree trunk, with his arms crossed. His eyes regarded her thoughtfully. Did she detect a smile hovering on his lips?

He laughed as he said, 'I thought I was asking her to marry me.'

Her doubts cleared away, Hazel walked up to him and putting her arms around him, kissed his lips and said, 'Of course I'd like to marry you, Jon.'

Hazel felt ecstatic and felt sure Jon did too as he kissed her passionately.

He produced a tiny leather-covered ring box from his pocket, and opening it, he took out a sparkling ring. Then taking her hand he slipped the ring on her finger.

It was official — they were engaged.

'Fancy you remembering to bring a ring!' she remarked, admiring her be-ringed hand.

'Susan prompted me to buy it for you before she left for London.'

They both laughed.

The distant owl reminded them, as the clock in the Cinderella story, that they must part and go home.

'I suppose you've already asked my parents if you could ask me to marry you?' Hazel enquired.

'Naturally! A Frenchman knows all about the art of love — gently persuading the lady he loves to marry him.'

'I had noticed — the red roses you gave me and a romantic setting for your proposal. What about French kissing?'

'Pleasures to come,' he chuckled.

We do hope that you have enjoyed reading this large print book.

Did you know that all of our titles are available for purchase?

We publish a wide range of high quality large print books including:
Romances, Mysteries, Classics General Fiction Non Fiction and Westerns

Special interest titles available in large print are:
The Little Oxford Dictionary Music Book, Song Book Hymn Book, Service Book

Also available from us courtesy of Oxford University Press:
Young Readers' Dictionary (large print edition) Young Readers' Thesaurus (large print edition)

For further information or a free brochure, please contact us at:
**Ulverscroft Large Print Books Ltd., The Green, Bradgate Road, Anstey, Leicester, LE7 7FU, England.
Tel:** (00 44) **0116 236 4325
Fax:** (00 44) **0116 234 0205**

THE SCOTTISH DIAMOND

Helena Fairfax

When actress Lizzie Smith begins rehearsals for *Macbeth*, she's convinced the witches' spells are the cause of a run of terrible luck. Her bodyguard boyfriend, Léon, is offered the job of guarding the Scottish Diamond, a fabulous jewel from the country of Montverrier. But the diamond has a history of intrigue and bloody murder; and when Lizzie discovers she's being followed through the streets of Edinburgh, it seems her worst premonitions are about to come true . . .

PLANNING FOR LOVE

Sarah Purdue

Mia Bowman has a plan for everything. Right now, her plan is to go to Crete, leaving all family distractions behind, and finish her first novel. This is her dream, and she has its achievement scheduled down to the last minute. Then she meets the handsome Alex, and starts to wonder whether everything in life can be planned for. Soon, Mia must decide whether to stick to her schedule or follow her heart . . .

DANGEROUS ENCOUNTER

Susan Udy

After Kate Summers witnesses a violent stabbing, she finds herself running for her life. Along with her two children, she moves to a small Cornish town, where they live quietly and anonymously as they try to start afresh. Then Kate encounters the handsome Ross St. Clair, and her life begins to change again. When she senses danger once more, she knows she has to keep herself and her children safe from harm. But how?